red
ant
house

red
ant
house

S T O R I E S

Ann Cummins

A Mariner Original

Houghton Mifflin Company

BOSTON • NEW YORK

For information about permission to reproduce
selections from this book, write to Permissions,
Houghton Mifflin Company, 215 Park Avenue South,
New York, New York 10003.

Visit our Web site: www.houghtonmifflinbooks.com.

Library of Congress Cataloging-in-Publication Data
Cummins, Ann.
Red ant house : stories / Ann Cummins.
p. cm.
"A Mariner original."
Contents: Red ant house—Trapeze—The shiprock fair—
Blue fly—Where I work—Crazy yellow—Headhunter—Dr.
War is a voice on the phone—The hypnotist's trailer—Bitter-
water—Starburst—Billy by the bay.
ISBN 0-618-26925-8
1. Southwestern States—Social life and customs—Fiction.
I. Title.
PS3603.U657R4 2003
813'.6—dc21   2002192153

Book design by Melissa Lotfy
Typefaces: Janson and Garage Gothic

Printed in the United States of America

QUM 10 9 8 7 6 5 4 3 2 1

Some of the stories in this collection appeared elsewhere
in slightly different form: "Headhunter" in *Hayden's Ferry Review;* "Billy by the Bay," "The Hypnotist's Trailer," and "Red
Ant House" in *McSweeney's;* "Bitterwater," "The Shiprock
Fair," and "Starburst" in *The New Yorker;* "Where I Work" in
A Room of One's Own; and "Dr. War Is a Voice on the Phone"
in *Sonora Review.*

For S.E.

Acknowledgments

Many thanks to Nancy Johnson, Steven Schwartz, and Tilly Warnock: best of readers and friends. To the Lannan Foundation, whose generous support gave me both the time to write and the confidence to continue. To Dave Eggers and the *McSweeney's* staff, who took a chance on my weirder stories. To Curtis Berkey, Sean Wilsey, and Dan Menaker, all of whom have been voices in the wilderness for my work. To Susan Canavan, an editor with an eye for the story under the story and the talent for calling it forth. And to my agent, Jenny Bent, a gracious, tenacious, wicked needler who makes things happen.

contents

red
ant
house

red ant house

The first time I saw this girl she was standing at the bottom of the coal pile. I thought she was a little wrinkled dwarf woman, with her sucked-in cheeks and pointed chin. She had narrow legs and yellow eyes. They had just moved into the old Perino house on West 2nd. This was the red ant house.

"I'm having a birthday," the girl said. She was going around the neighborhood gathering up children she didn't know for her birthday party. She told us they had a donkey on the wall and beans in a jar.

"What kind of beans?" I asked her.

She shrugged.

"Hey, you guys," I said to my brothers. "This bean wants us to go to her birthday party."

"My name's not Bean."

"What is it, then?"

"Theresa Mooney."

"You don't look like a Theresa Mooney."

She shrugged.

"Hey, you guys. This girl named Bean wants us to go to her birthday party."

She didn't say anything then. She turned around and started down the street toward her house. We followed her.

In her yard was a grease monkey. Her yard was a junker yard with car parts and cars all over the place, and a grease monkey was standing up against one car, smoking a cigarette.

"Joe," the little dwarf girl said, "what do you think of a name like Bean?"

He considered it. The man was handsome, with slick black hair and blue eyes, and he gave the dwarf a sweet look. I couldn't think of how such a funny-looking child belonged to such a handsome man. "It's an odd one," he said. The girl looked at me, her eyes slant. "One thing about a name like that," he said, "it's unusual. Everybody would remember it."

That idea she liked. She looked at me with a little grin. She said, "My name is Bean."

Just as if the whole thing was her idea.

Rosie Mooney was this Theresa's mother. When she moved in she had not known there would be ants in the house. These were the ants that had invaded the Perinos' chickens two summers before. Nobody wanted to eat chicken after that.

The ants came through the cracks in the walls. Rosie Mooney had papered those walls with velveteen flowered wallpaper. She had a red room and a gold room. She had wicked eyes to her, Rosie Mooney—could look you through and through.

These were trashy people, I knew. They had Christmas lights over the sink. They had hodgepodge dishes, and garlic on a string, and a book of matches under one table leg to make it sit straight. When the grease monkey came in, he kissed Rosie Mooney on the lips, a long wormy kiss, and then he picked the birthday girl up and swung her in a circle.

For us, he took off his thumbs.

"It is an optical illusion," the girl told us.

He could also bend his thumbs all the way back, tie his legs in a knot, and roll his eyes back and look at his brain.

"Your dad should be in the circus," I told the girl.

"He's not my dad."

"What is he?"

She shrugged.

The grease monkey laughed. It was a shamefaced laugh.

There were two prizes for the bean jar event: one for a boy, one for a girl. The boy's prize was a gumball bank. Put a penny in, get a ball of gum. When the gum was gone you'd have a bank full of pennies. Either way, you'd have something.

The girl's prize was a music box. I had never seen such a music box. It was black with a white ivory top made to look like a frozen pond, and when you wound it up, a white ivory girl skated over the top. It was nice.

We were all over that jar, counting the beans. It was me, my brothers, the Stillwell boys, the Murpheys, and the Frietags. As I was counting, I thought of something. I thought, *This jar is an optical illusion.* That was because there would be beans behind the beans. It occurred to me that there would be more beans than could be seen, thousands more.

The grease monkey was the official counter. He had written the exact number on a piece of tape and stuck it to the bottom of the jar. We all had to write our numbers down and sign our names. I wrote five thousand. When Joe read that, everybody laughed.

"There are beans behind the beans," I informed them.

"This one's a shrewd one," the grease monkey said. "She's thinking." But when he turned the jar over, the number on the tape said 730. This Joe winked at me. "Don't want to be thinking too hard, though."

I just eyeballed him.

"You want to count them? You can count them if you want," he said.

"I don't care to."

He grinned. "Suit yourself."

And he awarded the music box to the birthday girl, who had written 600. Then I knew the whole thing had been rigged.

The birthday girl's mother said, "Theresa, I bet you'd like some other little girl to have the music box since you have birthday presents. Wouldn't you?"

She didn't want to.

"That would be the polite thing," she said. "Maybe you'd like to give it to Leigh."

"I don't want it," I said.

This Theresa looked at me. She looked at the grease monkey. He nodded, then she held the box out to me.

But I didn't want it.

My mother was down sick all that summer. The doctor had prescribed complete bed rest so the baby would stay in. For the last three years, she had gone to bed again and again with babies that didn't take.

Up until that point, there were six of us children.

There was Zip, named for my grandmother, Ziphorah. Zippy loved me until I could talk. "You used to be such a sweet child," she would say. "We used to dress you up and take you on buggy rides and everybody said what a sweet child you were. Whatever happened to that sweet child?"

There was Wanda, named for my other grandmother. Wanda was bald until she was five, and my father used to take every opportunity to bounce a ball on her head.

There was me, Leigh Rachel, named by the doctor because my parents drew a blank. I'm the lucky one. Once when I was a baby I jumped out a window—this was the second-story window over the rock cliff. My mother, who was down sick at the time, had a vision about it. I was already gone. By the time she got herself out of her bed and up the stairs, I was in flight, but she leaped across the room, stuck her arm out, and caught me by the diaper, just as she'd seen it in the vision.

Another time, I survived a tumble down Bondad Hill in my grandpa's Pontiac. We both rolled like the drunk he was. Drunks I know about. My dad's dad was one, and my mom's dad was another. I never knew my dad's mom. She weighed three hundred pounds and died of toxic goiter. My mom's mom weighed seventy-five at the time of her death. Turned her face to the sky and said, "I despise you all." Irish like the rest of us.

There were the boys, Ronald Patrick, Raymond Patrick, Carl Patrick.

Then there were the ones who didn't take. One of these I saw, a little blue baby on a bloody sheet. My mother said, "Help me with these sheets," to Wanda, but Wanda couldn't stop crying, so I helped pull the sheet away from the mattress, and my mother wadded the sheet up.

I said, "We should bury that sheet."

She said, "It's a perfectly good sheet. We'll wash it."

Then she took a blanket and went into the living room and wrapped herself up in it. When my father came home he found her half bled to death.

My mother has Jewish blood in her. When they took her to the hospital, a Jewish man, Mr. Goldman, gave blood. He was the only Jew in town.

That summer my mother had cat visions. She would begin yelling in the middle of the night. She would come into our dreams: "The cats have chewed their paws off. They are under the bed."

"Mother, there are no cats."

"Look under the bed. See for yourself."

But we didn't want to.

Each day that summer I had to rub my mother's ankles and legs before I could go out to see the shadow, Theresa Mooney, who had started living in my backyard. When I woke up in the morning, there she was on the swing or digging in the ground with a spoon.

Once out of the house, I didn't like to go back. If I sneaked back in for any little thing, I had to rub the legs again. This was my job. Zip's job was to clean the house.

Wanda cooked. Grilled cheese on Mondays, frozen potpie on Tuesdays, Chef Boyardee ravioli on Wednesdays, frozen potpie on Thursdays, and fish sticks on Fish Fridays. Saturdays were hamburger and pork-and-bean days, and Sundays, Sick Slim brought trout that he caught in the river. Sick Slim had a movable Adam's apple and finicky ways. He used to exchange the fish for loaves of my mom's homemade bread until he found out that she put her hands in the dough. After that, he didn't care for bread, though he still brought the fish. "I never thought she would have put her hands in it," I heard him tell my father.

Slim was my dad's army buddy. He built his house on West 1st, way back from the street, right up against Smelter Mountain. Slim didn't want anybody at his back: that's what my dad said.

We knew a secret on him. My brother Ronnie saw this with his own eyes. A woman drove to West 1st where Sick Slim lived. She had a little blond girl with her, and when the girl got out of the car, Ronnie saw that she was naked. The mother didn't get out of the car. The little girl walked up that long sidewalk to the porch and up the steps to Slim's house and knocked on the door, and Slim opened the door, and he gave the girl money.

Slim was a bachelor and didn't have anything to spend his money on except naked children and worms for fish.

We all thought it would be a good idea to try and get some of Slim's money. My brothers thought I should take my clothes off and go up to his door, though I didn't care to. But I thought Theresa might like to make a little money, so I told her that there was a rich man on West 1st who would give us twenty dollars if she took her clothes off and walked up the sidewalk and knocked on his door. She didn't know about that. She was not accustomed to taking off her clothes outside.

I said, "Do you know how much twenty dollars is?"

She didn't know. She was as poor as a rat.

"You go first, then I'll go," she said.

"It's my idea." I figured if it was her idea—but she never had any—then she could say who went first.

"Mama says not to get chilled," she said. She was prone to sore throats and earaches and whispering bones. Without notice, she would go glassy-eyed and stiff, and would lose her breath. When she caught it again, she'd say, "My bones are whispering."

"What are they saying?" I'd ask.

"They don't talk," she said. "They don't have words. Just wind."

"You are a delicate flower," I said to butter her up.

She liked that.

"I bet we could get thirty dollars for you. You're better-looking than me."

She looked at me slant.

"It's easy," I said. "Don't think about it. You just think, *I am running through the sprinklers.* You don't think, *I am naked.* If you don't think about it, it's easy."

She told me she'd get beat if she took her clothes off outside.

"Maybe even forty dollars," I said, "because this particular gentleman likes itty-bitty things. Twenty for you, twenty for me. That's a lot of money. We could go places on that much money."

She thought about that. "I don't think we could go far on forty dollars."

"You got to look on the bright side. You're always looking on the dark side."

"No, I'm not."

"You are doom and gloom and whispering bones. Just ask your whispering bones. They'll say you're doom and gloom."

"You go first," she said. "Then I'll go."

"Maybe I will."

"Okay," she said.

"Okay then."

My mother was curious about Theresa and her mother. "Where does little Terry go when her mama's working?" my mother asked me. "If we had any room at all, I'd have that child here. If we weren't doubled up already."

"Hang her on a hook," I said.

"Don't smart-mouth. Do you think she would like to come here?"

Mother thought all children should like to come to our house because it was so pleasant to have a big family. To have children to do the cooking, and cleaning, and leg rubbing. Her legs were yellow logs. I didn't like to touch them, and so I would think of them as yellow logs at Cherry Creek—the dried logs split by lightning, with worm silk inside. I would close my eyes and rub the cold legs. Sometimes, if my mother didn't talk to me, if she only closed her eyes and breathed, I would forget I was in her room. I would put myself someplace else, Cherry Creek or Jesus Rock, and I would think of running my hands through soft things, the sand below Jesus Rock, or worm silk.

But, mostly, she talked. She wanted to know about Mooney and Joe. She wanted to know about Theresa.

When she talked she would sit propped up on pillows, her belly a world under the sheet. Her eyes were all glitter.

"She doesn't stay with that man, does she?"

"Joe Martin is his name."

"I don't care to know his name."

"I don't know where she stays."

My mother sighed. Except for the belly, she couldn't put weight on. She had trouble keeping food down, and she didn't have the strength to wash her hair so she kept it in a bandanna, one that bore the grease of her head.

"He has a wife and children, you know. Over in Dolores. I understand he has two little children. You mustn't say anything to the little girl, though. I'm sure she doesn't know. I understand," my mother said, "that he abandoned his family. I don't know how they make do.

"Now just look." She laughed and held her hands out to me. Her fingers were thick. The one ring finger was especially plumped out, and her wedding ring had sunk to the bone. "I have no circulation," she said, and she laughed again. They were cold, the fingers. "I'll be glad when this is over, Leigh. I guess we'll all be glad, won't we. Let's get some soap and get this ring off," she said.

I went for the soap and water. We soaped her hands good, and I started working the ring. She leaned back and closed her eyes. "Don't you love the sound?" she said.

"What sound?"

"Of the children playing. Listen to them." My brothers were kicking the can in the street. "You should be out, Leigh. Your poor old mom is all laid up, but you should be out. Why don't you go on out, now?"

"Shall I tell Mr. Richter he has to come and cut this ring off your finger?"

"Go on out," she said, "and tell little Terry what I told you." She opened her eyes and smiled. "I know you want to." An ugly smile.

"I'm not going to say anything."

She shook her head. "I was wrong to tell you. I don't know why I told you. It was very, very wrong of me. I would not have told you if I were myself. You understand that?"

"Yes."

She frowned and shook her head. "It's only natural that you should go tell her now. A child cannot keep such a secret."

"You want me to tell her?"

"Of course I don't want you to tell her. But you will."

"No, I won't."

"Yes, you will. You cannot keep a secret."

I didn't say anything. Just soaped the fingers.

"Leigh?"

"What?"

"Can you keep it a secret?"

"Yes."

"Look at me."

I looked at her.

We looked at each other for a long time. She took my chin. She pinched it. She was pinching it. "You are the one," she said, "who cannot keep a secret. Am I right?"

"I can," I said, but she was pinching it. She shook my head back and forth.

"Here," she said. She pulled the sheet back. She put my face against her belly. The baby was kicking. "Feel that?" she said. "That's your blood, too." She put her hand on my cheek and held my face there. The baby stopped kicking, and my mother laughed. "Well," she said, "it probably doesn't matter." She let me go. "It's just as well that little girl knows what kind of man is living under her roof."

"I can keep a secret."

She closed her eyes again and leaned her head against the wall behind her. She tried to twist the ring on her finger, but it wouldn't move. "I believe," she said, "we're going to have to cut this ring off. I cannot feel this finger anymore."

This was the summer they announced they were closing the mill. They were opening a new mill in New Mexico on an Indian reservation. Some workers got their walking papers. Some got transfers.

"What shall I do?" my father asked Wanda and me one night when we were walking down to the train depot. "Shall I take the transfer? Tell me what to do, and I'll do it."

We had to keep it secret because it was just the sort of news that would send my mother into a tizzy.

"It would mean a smaller house. You girls would all have to share one room, and the boys would have to share the other. But we'd eat good."

"What else could you do?" Wanda wanted to know.

He shrugged. "Collect the garbage?"

"You could do a lot of things," she said. She was against moving. Wanda was fourteen. She and Zippy had limbo parties for their friends in our living room. My brother Ronnie and I could out-limbo everybody because we were bendable beyond belief.

"You could work for the post office," Wanda said.

"I guess I could."

"Or the lumber mill."

"Mmm-hmm. Hate to let old Mike Reed down, though." Mike Reed was my father's boss. "That gentleman's done a lot for me. But I want to be fair to you kids, too. What do you think, Leigh?"

"Let's go."

"You'd have to leave all of your friends."

"That's okay."

"She doesn't have any friends," Wanda said.

"I do too."

"It's different if you're a little kid," she told my father.

"I think somebody's only thinking of herself," I said. He winked and took my hand. Wanda gave me a look.

"Good jobs are not that easy to come by," I said. My father squeezed my hand.

"We should put our fate in the hands of the Lord," I said.

He laughed. "Not bad advice," he said.

Wanda crossed her arms and just stared at the sidewalk in front of her.

On our way home we saw Joe at Lucky's Grill. We always stopped at Lucky's for ice cream on our way home. Joe was in a booth with a blond woman and two little boys. When he saw me a queer look came over him.

"That's the man who sniffs around Rosie Mooney," I said, "and I bet that's his wife and kids."

My father looked at Joe. "Wouldn't be the first time for old Joe Martin," he said quietly. He nodded and Joe nodded back.

"Mr. Martin, how you doing?" I called.

"I'm okay, Leigh. You?" The blond woman smiled. She was wearing red lipstick that made her look like she was all lips. That's how blond this woman was.

"Can't complain," I said. "I haven't seen Rosie and Theresa Mooney in a while, though." The blond woman kept smiling. She was smiling at her french fries.

"That old boy," I told my father when we got outside, "probably has a wife in every state. Don't you think?"

My father put his hands in his pockets. "You shamed him, Leigh."

"Joe?" I hooted.

He looked at me. "You shamed me," he said.

Wanda dug her elbow into me. "You shamed that man's wife," she said.

I dug her back.

"She shamed them, didn't she, Dad."

My father didn't say anything. He watched the air in front of him.

"God wouldn't spit you from his mouth," Wanda hissed.

Wanda's no saint. She'll knuckleball you in the back, and who are you going to scream to? The cats under the bed? The bloody cats?

Wanda's no saint, and Zip is no saint—*You used to be such a sweet child, we used to dress you up and take you in the buggy and everybody said what a sweet child you were, whatever happened to the sweet child?*

I'll tell you who's the saint. My father is the bloody saint. He'll say, "When I was over there in Guam? When I was fighting the Japansies? I walked to holy mass every day. I'd walk five miles if I had to. If it kilt me, I was going to holy mass."

So give the saint a hand.

The Bean was lying on our lawn, winding the music box. The skater skated. The Bean was keeping her finger on the skater's head, and the music was chugalugging because she was pressing the head too hard.

"My dad'd never leave my mom," I was telling her. "He's a good Catholic."

The Bean sucked her cheeks.

"This is why you want the holy sacrament of matrimony in the house. To keep 'em from leaving."

She wound up that music box. Everywhere she went, the music box went. Terry was addicted to the skater on the pond.

"Joe'll be back, though," I told her to give her comfort.

That morning, we had sat in the peach tree and watched Joe throw his clothes in the back of his truck while Rosie sat on the front porch and just smoked. "Don't you think?"

The Bean lay on her back and let the skater skate on her stomach. She closed her eyes.

"I mean, what'd he say? Did he say, 'I'm leaving you forever,' or did he say, 'I need time to think,' or did he say . . .'"

She was holding the skater, letting her go, holding her, letting her go, and the music was revving up just to stop, and I said, "Am I invisible?" Because she hadn't said a word all morning. "Are you a mute?" I said.

She looked at me for a minute, and then she screamed and laughed and the music box tumbled to the grass. "We're invisible!" she shouted. She flung her arms and legs out like an angel. "I'm a mute!" she yelled.

Then she started bawling. She said, "Don't look at me." She put her hands over her face and was bawling, a pitiful thing.

Me, I lay down next to her, and I didn't look at her, just lay there. The sky was blue-white. After a while she stopped bawling and started hiccupping. I said, "Got the chuck-a-lucks?" She sort of laughed and hiccupped. "You know the difference between chuck-a-lucks and hiccups?"

I felt something scratchy on my hand, and it was her withered little paw. She whispered, "Leigh, you are my best friend."

I thought of how skinny she was, and how she'd probably never find anybody to marry her. I held her dry hand and we started to sweat.

I said, "I know what'll cheer us up."

She said, "What?"

I let go her hand, rolled over on my side, and propped my head on my hand. I said, "That rich gentleman's money."

• • •

We both peed ourselves. I tried to hold it in but the Bean hot-footed down the sidewalk, did a little sidewinder dance, trying to keep her knees together, her pointy bottom shining, and the pee ran down, and I don't know if she was laughing or crying, but I was laughing so hard my stomach hurt. I peed his porch. Cars were honking. The Bean turned around and did a little dance for them, then scatted off around the house before we got the money. I pounded that door, and rang the bell. He was in there. The shades were open and then they closed. He was in there shaking in his boots.

After a while we went for our clothes, but then this car stopped at the curb, and this lady got out, yelled, "Hey!" We started running. I looked back, and the lady's my mom's friend, Mrs. Malburg, who made oily donuts and ate them, fat Mrs. Malburg: "Hey, Leigh!" She was standing on the curb looking at the bush where our clothes were. She shaded her eyes. She looked straight at us.

We hid in the little cave under Jesus Rock up there on Smelter Mountain. Theresa Mooney moaned, "I'm dead." She scrunched in the dirt, shivering up against the rock, and I didn't tell her there were ants there in the shadows. The year before I had buried a box of Cracker Jack there for a rainy day, but when the rainy day came and I dug them out, they were crawling with ants. I couldn't see Theresa Mooney's dirty feet where she was dug in. I didn't know if the ants were awake.

The Bean moaned, "I am dead, I'm dead, I'm dead." She said, "Will she tell?"

I started digging in the dirt with a stick. "Once," I told her, "there was an Indian maiden who got stole by the calvary, and when she ran away back to her tribe, they buried her naked in an ant pile and the ants ate her. Her own people did that."

"That's not true," Theresa Mooney said.

I shrugged.

"First of all," she said, "ants can't eat people."

"You don't know about all the species," I told her. "Sugar ants, no. But these were not sugar ants."

She didn't say anything to that.

A train whistle was blowing—the Leadville train coming in. It was five o'clock. By now, my dad would be home. He'd be sitting at the kitchen table with his boots unlaced, stirring his coffee. Wanda'd be taking the potpies out of their boxes.

"Will she tell?" the Bean whispered.

Mrs. Malburg, muddy-eyed Mrs. Malburg, would be sitting across the table from my dad, giving him trouble. They would be talking in whispers so my mother wouldn't hear. "It is," I said, "against human nature to keep a secret."

The Leadville train whistled again. It was probably pulling into the depot.

I closed my eyes and listened hard.

"I'm cold," the Bean whispered.

"You can wrap yourself around me like a spider monkey," I told her. "I don't mind."

She crawled from the back of the cave and wrapped her ice-cube self around me. She said, "You smell like yellow urine."

"So lick me," I said, and the Bean laughed.

I was listening for my brothers, who would be coming after us. Wanda would send them. She would say, *Jesus wouldn't spit you from his mouth*. They would all say it. "The calvary is coming," I told the Bean. "Mark my word."

"We're dead," the Bean said.

"We are dead under Jesus Rock," I yelled so they'd know where to look.

"Shh!" the Bean hissed.

"This is Lazarus's cave!"

She unwrapped herself and scowled at me. She crawled to the edge of the hole, knelt there looking out, her little bottom tucked under her filthy heels. She stood up and stepped out into the sun. She stretched on her tiptoes and looked down the mountain. She turned around, her face twitching to go.

I crawled out, too. The evening breeze had a sting, and the sun was sitting on the mountain. Scrub oak leaves were crackling all around.

"Nobody's coming," she whispered. She squinted down the path.

"That," I said, "is an optical illusion."

At the bottom of the hill in the back of Sick Slim's house, a light went on, and then Sick Slim was standing at the window, looking up Smelter Mountain. We scatted back into the hole. Terry started giggling and whimpering. "He saw us," she said. "We're trapped."

"Him?" I hooted. "He's blind." Then I remembered what my dad had said, how ever since he got back from playing soldier, Sick Slim didn't like anybody at his back. But we *were* at his back. Two naked children. I laughed.

"What?" the Bean said.

I crawled back out into the sun. I stood up and walked to the edge where he could see me good. I put my hands on my hips like King of the Mountain. I couldn't see his face, couldn't see him looking, but I knew he was.

I said, "Next time, we'll *make* him give us money."

"How?" the Bean said.

I didn't know exactly how. It was coming to me. It was a dream in the distance.

trapeze

The Bureau of Indian Affairs did three good things this one
year: they got us band uniforms, gymnastics equipment,
and releases from class for special assemblies every third
Friday. So every third Friday we trooped down to the cafeteria
with its pink walls and gummy floor to watch exotic acts. In
September we got quilters from the Baptists' quilting bee,
three women who told us the history of America in quilt pat-
terns, and in October Farmington's volunteer fire department
showed us how they trained their dogs. But in November we
got a hypnotist. A hypnotist!

He drove up during third period, and we watched him un-
roll himself from his Ford pickup. He was a long, lanky specimen dressed in black: a Stetson on his head, Tony Lamas on
his feet. Mr. Lawson said, "Time passes, people. Will you?"
We were just staring. The hypnotist was a handsome man!

This was unexpected. In that little corner of the reservation,
we were unaccustomed to handsomeness among adults. None
of our teachers was handsome, not big-eyed Mr. Lawson, who
penciled in the bald spots of his little mustache, and not Miss

Adams, the bull-legged, square-bodied P.E. teacher—she had this whinny in her voice—and not fat Mr. Bellows, the history teacher, though we all liked him, especially when he propped his feet on the desk, leaned back in his chair, went to sleep, and then fell over. There was one handsome adult in town, the state trooper, Officer Chris, King of the Bloody Thirty, the thirty-mile stretch of road leading off the reservation. Now and again he invited us kids to look at pictures of accident victims. The pictures made our eyes pop.

After lunch, we trooped into the cafeteria, which was also the girls' gym. They'd rolled out the bleachers on one side of the room and put down brown paper over the sticky floor. In the center of the room there was a pile of rope. The hypnotist sat in a folding chair next to it. He was wearing this green swami hat instead of the Stetson, though he still had on the Tony Lamas. He looked us over, and he looked interested. He had this little smile. A curious eyebrow climbed high on his forehead when he looked at our varsity cheerleaders in their Friday getups, the cherry and gray cheerleading skirts. They sat in the front row, their knees pressed together.

I hadn't yet figured out how to be popular, but I was working on it. My brother, Ronnie, was advising me. "Say hi in the halls," he was always telling me. He said hi in the halls like a roving politician, and he got elected: band president, student council president, basketball co-captain.

Before we moved to the reservation, we lived in this big Victorian house in Colorado, where I was mostly invisible. I'm the fifth of seven kids. "Our little pill has to raise her hand if she wants to get a word in edgewise," Mama liked to say every time I opened my mouth at the dinner table. "Quiet, everybody, the little pill wants to speak."

I liked the dark places in that old house. I liked sitting on the staircase between the first and second floors. This was a windowless place with plaster walls, a door at the bottom, and a little brown fence at the top for baby safety. Light sifted down from the bedroom where Ronnie liked to parachute my underwear out the window, and below, in the kitchen, Mama clanged pots, reminding us that she hates to cook. The staircase was my secret place. I liked sitting in the shadows, watching the roof where it sloped to the door and thinking about trapezes.

I saw only the trapeze and me on it, holding the bar between the bend of my knee or in the arch of my foot. A long-roped trapeze, thousands of feet long with no floor below or ceiling above. It would swing me lazily—I loved the feel—through black space. I could stay in sync with the moving rope, make my muscles reach their greatest stretch when the trapeze slowed to its peak, flip off at the last possible moment, and curl myself into a roll. I could roll twenty times in twenty somersaults before it was time to catch the next trapeze.

To sit between floors and flip to the beat of clanging pots—that was what I liked best about that old house. On the reservation, we got a company house, a tiny gray three-bedroom box that looked exactly like all the other company boxes, and outside our window we had what Mama called the Wasteland—miles and miles of sand.

I missed that old house. Truth be told, though, I didn't mind the Wasteland. I loved riding shotgun in the car with the window open, the hot, dry air rushing past me, dreaming of Nancy Drew, whom I imagined gliding along next to me in her red convertible, a white scarf around her neck, a victory laugh on her face, blind to the sagebrush she crushed and the gullies she leapt. She'd dip in and out of dry washes, skip prickly pears, dodge hogans and sheepdogs and telephone poles. I liked to imagine my bike was hooked to the back of her car and she'd whiz me along with her. I had fat tires that could easily handle the heat, and I'd roll over rattlesnake heads, zoom up utility poles to follow the electric wires.

I figure-eighted thousands of miles over dry desert, skidded through lizards and scorpions and tarantulas, barreled head-long toward fat birds on telephone poles, jumped ditches, zig-zagged canyons—it wasn't so bad.

What I didn't have, though, after three years on the reservation, was friends, and I was in danger of becoming—maybe already was—a dork.

During assembly, we stomped up the wooden bleachers and Mr. McGilly growled at us through the microphone, "Quiet, please, softly, please," and, "If you're chewing gum and I find it on the floor there'll be no more assemblies." The senior boys always grabbed the top row against the wall. They me-owed and hissed—"Shhht"—and threw sunflower hulls as we marched in.

There were rules for assemblies, which we broke every time. Number one rule: Clap. We had been warned. Monday morning after the quilters and then after the firemen, Mr. McGilly took fifteen minutes on the intercom: "You want to make our guests feel welcome, don't you? You like getting out of class, don't you?" Sometimes the cheerleaders clapped, and we all watched them. Sometimes my brother marched back and forth with his band baton, raised the baton as if to orches-trate clapping, and we all laughed because he was popular, but we didn't clap. I don't know why.

When the show was about to start, Mr. McGilly got up on his tiptoes and clutched the microphone. "Ladies and gentle-men," he shouted, his eyes bulging, "let's hear a warm round of applause for Mystic Michael Hurt." The microphone squawked. Mystic Mike put his arms over his head as if dodg-ing a hurricane, dug into his ear, and we all laughed, and the cheerleaders clapped.

• • •

Mystic Mike did rope tricks. "Now watch the circle," he said. He made a lasso out of the rope and stood twirling circles at his feet. "If you can concentrate," he said, "if you can watch the circles without blinking, say the way a cat—" He had this deep agreeable voice, like a priest's. I watched the circles loop and wobble in front of him, then to one side, then the other, big sloppy Os that skimmed the surface of the floor, skimmed, skimmed, slapped hard like a jump rope, then skidded. Stopped dead in a wad at his feet. The boys behind me went, "Ya-eee." "Just watch the rope," Mystic Mike warned, his voice changing to a throaty bark. I guess those guys'd seen better rope tricks. Me too, but Michael Hurt was so handsome! I watched him jerk his hips and head, getting the circles started again.

I half-closed my eyes until his lasso began to wind in blurry, smooth circles, and I thought of how sweet it would be if a handsome hypnotist held my trapeze. I'd never worried myself over how the trapeze ropes were fixed, but something had to hold them. Or somebody, and I figured it would be fine if this gentleman hovered in the clouds above, like Jack the Giant— or no. Like Geppetto. Who would look like this guy. Like Mike. Somewhere above me in deep space, a giant puppeteer might chant in a deep, priesty voice, and I probably wouldn't understand the words: they'd be spiritual sounds—

"Hypnotism is simply deep concentration."

—the ropes laced through his fingers, and as I pumped, he might give me a little push, a finger twitch, that would send me arcing wider and wider, higher and higher. I'd understand him in my heart, not my head—

"Animals," he said, "go into trances all the time. Pigs. Horses. Coyotes." Mystic Mike. I didn't like his name. Mystic Michael. Why Michael? It was so plain. He was chewing his lip and talking at the same time. "They have greater access to altered states than we, but some of us, a special few, retain this tremendous connection to the waking dream." He let the rope drop at his feet. He began looking us over, turning his head slowly from side to side, stopping now and again to squint at somebody, a little smile on his lips. My heart started thudding when his eyes stopped at me. I held my breath and waited for him to look away. He didn't. He just stared at me!

I didn't want to be hypnotized. I didn't know exactly what it would mean, but probably it'd mean standing up in front of everybody, which I couldn't do. All of a sudden I can't breathe, and my hands are wet, cold, and a lump's in my throat, like vomit or something'll come out if I open my mouth. He won't look away. He's saying, "Ten percent of the population is highly vulnerable. While we've been talking I have suggested, well, other ways of being. Subliminally. If you're one of the ten percent, you will do whatever I want you to do." Did he want me to do something? He drew his hands together under his chin. He looked like he was witching me! "I want you all to be very, very quiet." He began rocking back and forth from heels to toes.

He said, "Horse."

I stared at this girl's braid in front of me. It was a thick, snaky gob of hair.

He stamped. He said it again.

Behind me somebody was laughing. Out of the corner of my eye, I saw this kid stand up. It was Hayden Kramer. Tossing his head, little Hayden, the typing teacher's kid, no bigger than I was, but a junior, a middling-popular red-haired pipsqueak—neighing. "Come on down here," Mystic Mike said. "Shh," he said, because a lot of kids were laughing, but Hayden went on down and started trotting, tossing his red mane. The boys behind me kissed the air.

"Rooster," the hypnotist said, and up jumped Leonard Kotaceet, the sophomore class president. Leonard was crowing. Put his fists into his armpits, flapped his wings, and practically fell trying to get to the floor. Then my brother turned into a cow. I could tell by the way his mouth was twitching—Ronnie wanted to laugh.

So he was faking it. The act was rigged. My ears stopped thudding so bad. I watched Linda Bitsui, one of the three Navajo cheerleaders, start to purr, and Randi Rouseau, one of the white ones, started barking, and I wondered if I'd always be a dork. Everybody around me was laughing, nudging each other, like what a good joke, like they'd been in on it all along.

Mystic Mike raised a nice little zoo. Before the show was half over he was herding a pig from student council, a duck from the honor society, and a first-string bulldog from the football team, all oinking and quacking and barking and laughing, a very popular zoo, probably handpicked and coached by Mr. McGilly from a list he'd jotted down of everybody who was anybody—a list I'd never be on. When Mr. McGilly looked at me, he got this silly smile, like he was wracking his brain, thinking, *Who's this specimen?* Like, *I should know this girl* . . . , and he always said, "Hi there" instead of "Hi, Karen." I bet I'm the only white kid in that school whose name he never remembered.

Mystic Mike was beaming right at me. The faker. He didn't even see me.

Like Moses, he shivered his hands over the zoo, and the animals screeched their noises, and he shouted, "Owl." Nothing happened so he shouted again, motioning the herd to pipe down, but nothing happened. He stamped, boomed, "Owl!"

A voice to the left of the bleachers said, "That's me." I craned my neck. It was Purple! She stood up, stepped down the rows onto the floor, her hands in the pockets of her sweater. She was grinning at her friends, waving inside her pocket, and I'm thinking, *She's on Mr. McGilly's list?* Because Purple was not popular, not with Mr. McGilly. Then I remembered she was the student council representative from

Soph. Level 2. The others on the floor were all Level 1s. You got put in a level based on how good your English was, though the way I saw it, it wasn't that Purple didn't have good English. I believe the teachers thought she had too much of it. She was a troublemaker. She had a reputation. She said, "Who." Said it flatly, not at all like an owl. Then she said, "Ya-eee," and grinned. All the girls where she was sitting started clicking their tongues. "Who," she said. "Ya-eee." Mystic Mike rolled his eyes. She stopped in front of the zoo, faced us, and took a little bow. Some kids clapped. Then Mystic Mike bowed, too.

They called her Purple because of the purple sweater she always wore. I'd made her acquaintance three years earlier, our first year on the reservation. I was walking home from school, taking the shortcut behind the band building. Then, the sweater swam around her hips. It still did because she tugged it down, but now there were holes where the yarn had pulled loose at the shoulders and collar. That day behind the band building, she taught me something: Indian girls will hit you. This amazed me. She said, "What would you do if I socked you in the stomach?" And then did.

Right away I thought, *Tell Mom*. Mama was gathering evidence that first year to justify marching us off the reservation. She wanted us back in civilization, which meant Catholic schools. There were Catholic boarding schools for Indian kids, but none for us. "You're a smart man," she told my dad every night. "You can get other jobs."

Then again, telling Mom things didn't always work out so well. That was also the year Ronnie decided to get holy. Until then he'd always been a go-along Catholic. He'd go with us to mass if he didn't get a better offer. But this one day, out of the blue, he announced that his new mission in life was to light a fire under the Catholic Youth Organization. My mom's eyes went all soft when he said this, like he had read her mind and said the one thing she'd been praying hardest for. Ronnie was in ninth grade then. He spent hours in front of the mirror, smearing his hair with VO-5 and then parting it this way and that. He told me that Catholic girls are sex-starved and the reason so many joined CYO is because they got to do the hug of peace in Jesus' name. He told me he planned to be there for all those sex-starved nymphos, to let them rub up against him just as long as they wanted, and that I'd better plan to take over all the chores because he had a lot of CYO business to take care of. Sure enough, he started skipping out right after dinner—I don't think he did a dish all year, and he was never around for Saturday chores. I tried to tell Mom exactly why he was so interested in CYO—"Sex. He told me so!"—and she looked sour. "If, indeed, your brother told you this, I'm sure he didn't intend you to tell me. You don't want to grow up to be a snitch, do you, Karen?"

You never knew how something would hit her. So I didn't tell her about Purple. That night, I played it over and over in my head. Purple'd been standing in the shade with her cousin, Lily. I said, "Hi." She said the thing about socking me in the stomach. I kept walking, but I watched her face. First there was the idea, then, an instant later, the decision. I'm gasping and she's squinting at me, her fists clenched. Then she crossed her arms like some kind of prizefighter, and there was this gleam in her eye, and I knew what she was thinking. She was thinking, *Yes, I do dare punch a hole through this scared little white girl in her corduroy coveralls and saddle shoes and pin-curled hair. Yes, I'd be pleased to roll this little puff of kitten fur in the dirt.*

I believe she was the first Navajo to really notice me, and I guess the only one to go really deep—from the rim of my belly button to the mole on my spine. I waited to see what would happen next, but then Purple went away. I heard they sent her to boarding school in Kansas. But that was three years ago.

• • •

Purple and I weren't the same size—I don't care that the scales read ninety-three pounds for both of us and that the metal measuring stick resting on the tops of our heads showed our heights to be fifty-eight inches exactly. She was not my size. Stand us next to each other in our P.E. costumes—they were these baby-blue one-piece button-down gizmos, short sleeves and a metal Wonder Girl belt at the waist, with folds of cotton ballooning out and then gathering in tight elastic that left lines of pink dashes on our legs—stand us next to each other under a spotlight in the center of the gym, and Purple would cast the larger shadow.

Miss Adams didn't see it that way. "You girls are exactly the same size," she announced. "You'll spot each other." This was a couple of days after Purple did her owl impersonation. The custodians had just put up the uneven bars for gymnastics. I had decided I would try out for the new gymnastics team, since the BIA was so nice to buy us the equipment and all. Trying out for some team was on my "to do" list that fall, along with saying hi in the halls. I had also decided I would speak up in class at least once a week. I was doing great at that one. Each Friday, when Mr. Bellows assigned the weekend homework, I raised my hand and asked him to repeat himself. He always obeyed, right there in front of everybody, which was cool. For half a minute every Friday afternoon, I was a star.

I almost backed out when I saw Purple among the would-be gymnasts, but then I thought, *That's exactly what I always do, back out*, and I was sick of doing what I always did, so I stuck around that first day. We learned how to do round-offs on the mats, and I was pretty good at it. I just kept my distance from her, and she stuck with her cousin, and everything was fine. We spent the first three weeks tumbling around on the mats, and we spent the next on the balance beams, but for the bars we had to have spotters, and oh, lucky me.

"Now don't be shy, girls," Miss Adams said. She had me stand barefoot on a padded mat. She had Purple kneel behind me. "Karen, fall backwards, and Evangeline will catch you." Evangeline was Purple's real name. I couldn't fall backwards. "Just relax," she said, and pushed me in the chest, and I stepped back on Purple's leg.

"Ow!" she said.

"Sorry," I said.

"This is easy," Miss Adams said. "You have to be Loosey Goosey if you want to be a good tumbler. Remember, girls," she said, and there was that whinny in her voice, "you won't break." She had Purple put her arms across my back, and she told me not to bend my knees, and she pushed me. I looked in Purple's eyes. They were perfectly bland brown eyes. I was thinking, *She doesn't remember me.*

All period, we fell into each other's arms, and we were sort of laughing, and it wasn't so bad. Later, in the locker room, Purple and Lily stood in front of the mirrors, ratting their hair. "Now, don't be shy," Purple said to the mirror. "Ya-eee."

Lily said, "You have to be Loosey Goosey."

Everybody was cracking up because Miss Adams was such a dork, and I was thinking, *Say hi in the halls.* Before I could talk myself out of it, I said, "Remember, girls. You won't break."

I was sitting on a bench behind them, tying my shoes. Purple looked at me in the mirror, and I saw this hardness come into her eyes. She was watching me, her eyes narrow and evil. She smiled, and she began to nod very slowly. She said, "You *might* break," and I knew from the gleam in her eye that I was the *you* she was talking about. If she hadn't remembered me before, she did now, and I didn't know why I'd opened my fat mouth.

In my mind, I saw myself boomerang up from the low bar, reach back for an eagle grasp of the high, and I felt my fingers cramp, unable to curl around the steel; I watched myself drift down toward her chalky hands, hands that disappeared, and I listened for the splat.

She said, "Remember. The spotter's responsibility is to break the fall, not the back." She grinned at Lily.

I knew I'd better watch out.

Purple came into the trading post that Saturday. I had a little weekend job measuring cloth and selling jewelry in the dry goods section. Purple was with an old woman. I'd often see her walking around town with this woman. The woman dressed traditional, long tiered cotton skirt, velvet blouse. Tennis shoes, a bandanna over her gray hair. I figured she might be Purple's grandmother. She wore turquoise bracelets from wrists to elbows, and a huge squash blossom around her neck, a heavy necklace that dragged her toward the ground. She was stooped, a tiny woman, her face all wrinkly.

When Purple saw me, she squinted. They breezed by, back to the rug room, where I heard the trader, Mr. Slaugh, say, "Ya'at'eeh shimah"—hello, my mother—which was what he said to every old woman who came into the store, and always made me think of the time the vacuum cleaner salesman came to our house in Colorado and said, "Hello, Mom," to my mother, and she slammed the door in his face, yelling, "*I* am *not* your mother." But the Navajo women had rugs, and Mr. Slaugh was there to buy.

Mr. Slaugh stocked bolts of stiff, waxy cloth that he sold for forty-nine cents a yard, and I spent most of my Saturdays measuring yards and yards of it, colorful, printed cloth that people bought to throw over sweathouses for ceremonies. That was what I was doing when Purple came and draped herself across the glass jewelry counter, smudging it—I sprayed that counter with Windex a hundred times a day—and said, pure spit in her voice, "What are you doing here?"

"Working."

She stood there glaring at me, as if what I was doing was a personal insult to her. I could hear the old woman talking in Navajo to Mr. Slaugh.

I tried to cozy up to her. I whispered, "The Mormons are trying to brainwash me."

She didn't smile; the sneer did not leave her face, so I didn't go on. It was true, though. The reason I had the job, a good job for an underage kid, was because my employers were bribing me. I'd proven my reliability. I had babysat for the Slaughs, good Mormon traders, for the past three years. I was a good babysitter and let the kids bite me. They wanted me to come and live with them—to be their live-in babysitter and go on vacations with them to exotic places.

"Over my dead body," my mother said. My mother did battle with Mormon missionaries on a regular basis. Every few weeks, a couple of white-shirted, clean-faced Mormon boys came onto the company compound. We were mostly Catholics, Baptists, and Church of Christers. The missionaries would say their how-do-you-dos and ask for glasses of water all around the block, and the Protestants, who were generally polite, sometimes gave them cookies. My mother, on the other hand, met them at the door, and while she didn't carry a baseball bat or gun, she might as well have. "God save the Navajo people from the likes of you," she'd say, right to their faces, and she explained to them in no uncertain terms about how Jesus built his true church, the Catholic Church, on Peter the Rock, our first pope, but you didn't see his ambassadors, the priests, going door to door like vacuum cleaner salesmen. The missionaries seemed to like this. They'd plant their feet, open their mouths, and match her point for point. They always spent hours longer at our house than any other, and they never got cookies or water. As far as my mother was concerned, she always won because they always left.

She liked a good fight. She spent hours comparing numbers

in the various churches, scheming about how to beat the Mormons by upping the Catholic ranks among the Navajo. She saw us kids as soldiers in the field. While I wasn't the little crusader Ronnie turned out to be, I never quarreled about going to mass or confession. I believe my mother let me work for Mormons because she liked putting her little soldier in the line of fire, just to show the enemy what true faith was.

But Purple's face told me she had no interest in any of this. We had dead pawn in the case she leaned on. She watched me measure cloth for a while, and then decided to be interested in pawned jewelry. "Let me see this," she said, poking the glass.

I got the key, opened the case, and took out a tray of old rings.

"These are for sale?" she asked. She picked out a ring with a green turquoise stone that looked like the world with all its seas. "How long you had this one?" It swam on her finger, covering joint to knuckle.

"I don't know. Couple of months."

She picked up the little white tag and looked at the price. She said, "This is my uncle's ring."

"Oh?"

She took the ring off and looked at its underside. "He's been looking for it," she said. "Who brought it here?"

I shrugged. Every now and again, Mr. Slaugh toted in a bunch of stuff from the pawned goods and put it in the sales case. I'd been there, though, when people came in and saw things they'd pawned up for sale. I saw this one man get so mad that when he rushed out of the room, he sideswiped a display of tomato paste in the grocery section and sent a pile of four-ounce cans flying. Another time, a woman refused to leave the store. She sat down in the middle of the floor and stayed there—all day. Mr. Slaugh had gone to Gallup. None of us could do a thing. I don't know what happened that time. I was just a flunky and got to leave when my shift was over.

"My uncle didn't pawn this," Purple informed me. "How can you sell something that doesn't belong to you?"

I told her she was going to have to talk to Mr. Slaugh about it because I was just a flunky, and she said, "I'm going to take this ring back to my uncle." She closed it in her fist and put the fist in the pocket of her sweater.

The whirlies started in my stomach. I said, "Somebody pawned it," but she was already heading out, though at the door she stopped and looked back. Her upper lip curled and I again saw the prizefighter behind the band building. I knew what she was thinking: *Are you a little snitch? Go on and tell, snitch, so I can despise you even more.* I didn't move, just stared back.

It was a two-hundred-dollar ring. Mr. Slaugh winked at petty theft. Kids stole licorice under his nose, or they popped the tops on their Nehis, drank them while wandering the aisles. He liked to be generous. "Did you pay for that?" he'd ask the thief, and the thief would stare off somewhere, and Mr. Slaugh would say, "Well, you pay for it next time" and then go off all pleased with himself.

Real theft was a whole other thing. For real theft he called the butcher, a meaty guy named Albert, and Albert pinned the thief while Mr. Slaugh called the cops. The cops came with handcuffs and took the thief to the jail, which was just on the other side of the fence from the company compound. Summers, we lined up at the fence with crab apples and pelted the cops in their paddy wagons, then hid in our houses and watched them tour the block, looking for us. I could just see it: The paddy wagon drives up, the Navajo cop gets out, walks around and opens the back door. Purple, in handcuffs, jumps out. For Purple, Mr. Slaugh'd surely call the Navajo cops, whereas if it were, say, me—if they could prove the ring went missing on my shift, and if I couldn't lie, and if I couldn't tell

the truth either, if I zipped my lip and swallowed my tongue—
Mr. Slaugh would call Officer Chris, the handsome state
trooper, because I'm white, and for whites you always called
the state troopers first. Our parents warned us all about that: *If
you get into trouble, call a state trooper; the Navajo cops have no ju-
risdiction over you.*

There were worse things, I guessed, than riding in the back
of that handsome cop's car. Officer Chris, his dark eyes in the
rearview, those sad, sweet eyes full of concern: *The reason you
kids don't want to drink and drive is because you could end up just a
statistic on the Bloody Thirty. Do you want that? No, sir. All right,
then.* Full of concern, those eyes, for kids driving through the
Wasteland. Riding in the back seat of his car might not be so
bad. Plus, everybody'd see me in a new light. Would I be popular then? The little pill's in jail. "It's always the quiet ones,"
they'd say.

In truth, it made me feel creepy. I couldn't bear to be noticed in that ugly way. What would Officer Chris think? He
would think I was a child, or stupid—to let a thief walk out the
door in the bright daylight and never say a word. Or Mr.
Slaugh. He wouldn't want me around his store, and he surely
wouldn't want me around his kids. To be *fired*! When I
thought of my mother, her horror when she heard the Mormons let me go, it made my stomach hurt.

That Monday, Purple wore the ring to school. She showed it
to Lily and Tyrone in the cafeteria. Tyrone was Purple's
boyfriend and the star point guy on the varsity basketball
team. She knew how to get in with the popular kids. She was
always getting Tyrone in trouble. They made out everywhere—in the halls, in the cafeteria, on the bus—and were always getting called into Mr. McGilly's office for grossing
everybody out.

Anyway, she came in that Monday, and she was wearing her

sweater, jeans, boots, and these bright orange gloves, which she began to remove slowly, very slowly—it was a procedure. Hand in the air, finger by finger, she took off the right, wiggled her fingers for all to see, then started on the left, the knitted pinky, the ring, the middle, inching each halfway off, moving very deliberately like a magician—like, *Guess what I have in the palm of my hand?*—then whipped the thing off, and Presto! There was the ring on her middle finger, half of it wrapped in red yarn to make it fit. She held it out for Lily and Tyrone to admire.

Just in case I hadn't noticed, she made a big deal of it at practice. While the rest of us gathered around Miss Adams for our instructions, Purple cartwheeled back and forth across the mat, the ring orbiting her, and she couldn't seem to hear Miss Adams call her. Ten minutes later, I was standing at the uneven bars, waiting for her to spot me. She came walking over, twisting the ring. Said, "I don't think I can get this thing off. It's stuck."

"I thought it was your uncle's," I said.

She grinned. "He let me borrow it."

I wanted to smash her.

Every day that week she wore the ring and wanted to talk about it. I couldn't stand to look at her ugly face.

On Saturday, Mr. Slaugh held an employee meeting. He'd done a preliminary inventory, getting ready for the end-of-year count. He wanted to know if we knew what slippage was, then told us. "Missing inventory. A store can tolerate some slippage, but it looks to me like we might be as high as eight percent this year. Eight percent, people!" He was especially concerned about the high-priced items, the jewelry, the sand paintings, the quality hats. He wondered if he needed to supervise these items himself, though he didn't see how he could. He was just one man. "That's why I hired you," he told us. He looked each of us in the face—there were the two cashiers, Mae and Alice, the grocery stocker, David, the bookkeeper, Lois, Albert, and me. My face started to get hot. I tried to remember who else was around when Purple had pulled her little caper. Had anybody else seen? I couldn't remember anything about that morning but her. "I have faith in you," Mr. Slaugh said. "You're good, Christian people, every one."

I was the only non-Mormon employee. He was looking at Mae, then at me, then Mae again, then—I tried to meet his eyes. There were red veins in the whites. He wasn't looking away. He had this fixed look, like he was trying to read my mind. He was boring a hole right through me!

I said, *Karen is invisible.* I said it silently. With my mind, I said it. I didn't look at the red veins. I looked at the blank spot in the middle of his forehead. I said it over and over without making a sound: *Karen is invisible. Karen is invisible. Karen is invisible.*

He said he was going to put up a box. If anybody had any suggestions about where he might look for lost items—"Eight percent, people!"—he or she should please put a little note in the box, anonymous was fine, no questions asked.

Karen is invisible.

I dreamt about trapezes in the middle of the afternoon. I couldn't help it. I used to do this all the time, anywhere, until blink, here's Mama shaking me, yelling, "Can't you hear me talking to you?" I don't like people spying on me, so I tried to pay attention and only dream when I was alone, but then all of a sudden, right in the middle of history, I looked outside the window, out across the field of yellow weeds, out where Mr. Neskahi's hobbled horses stood, their breath visible in the cold, and from the sky, a trapeze floated, skimming the horses' bent backs, just a little bit, barely grazing those old horses.

Like some kind of light-footed horsefly, my trapeze came to get me, and before I knew it I was soaring through the blue-white cold of the winter sky. Out beyond the river, up and over the bluff, past the graveyard, that old raggedy place with its rotting graves, out to clean, bare sand. My ears closed up, and my eyes went dead, and I never heard the bell ring, and didn't even see kids get up and go, and then Mr. Bellows was standing right there, shaking me, asking me if I was asleep, which was so embarrassing.

I scatted on out of there, and I almost didn't go to practice. Almost, I talked myself out of it, but Miss Adams always checked the absence list and always made a big production when somebody skipped practice. I didn't want a big production, so like some kind of zombie I went ahead and went, where I had to look at Purple and listen to her, and I couldn't stand that.

Ronnie had an opinion about Purple: "She's a sex-starved exhibitionist," he said. He, on the other hand, was what he called a calculating opportunist, which meant he knew how to seize the moment and make it work for him. He planned to seize the moment when it came, and skedaddle on out of the "rat hole." "Here," he said, "we're big fish. But on the outside, we're nothing." College would have to be his ticket off the reservation. He couldn't count on academic scholarships because a good GPA in our school was a joke, and no way were we prepared for college entrance exams. He planned to rely on charm, good looks, and connections. He already had glowing recommendation letters from his coaches, and Mr. McGilly was going to call an old fraternity brother who was president of the Colorado School of Mines. Mr. McGilly promised he'd get in there—with money.

Dorks, on the other hand, didn't have a prayer. "You gotta get noticed, make some noise," Ronnie advised, "but it's got to be the right noise, in the right place, at the right time," which was the key to being a calculating opportunist, but not an exhibitionist.

"She makes me sick," he said about Purple. As far as he was concerned, she was single-handedly destroying the varsity basketball team's chances of going to state because of her exhibitionism, which was also robbing him of a chance to be seen by college scouts who went to the state tourneys. Ronnie wasn't a bad basketball player, but he was nothing next to Tyrone, who had been put on "official notice" for "inappropriate displays of affection."

"It's not Tyrone's fault," Ronnie said. "He wasn't like that before she came. She'll do anything to get attention."

He didn't know the half of it.

Every day, Purple cooked up some new torture for me. She was smart in that way. It's like she walked into my head and poked around and found my secret-desire room. I mean, she noticed things other people didn't. Poked around in there, thinking, *What does this white girl like?* then, *Oh, looky here:* I think she knew how much I liked the uneven bars. Swinging on them—it's the closest I got to a real trapeze. So Purple, she figured out how to mess that up for me.

It was just after Christmas break. Miss Adams sat us down and gave us a little lecture. Said she was generally disappointed in us. "You're miserable." She wanted to know why, after nearly nine weeks, our joints were still jelly. "Excellence, girls, is an attitude. Failure is an attitude, too. If you believe you're failures, you will be. Single-minded devotion to the sport, that's what you need to be an athlete. No distractions. When you're in this room, you think about the sport. You don't think about boys, you don't think about the Twinkies you had for breakfast. You visualize the movements, and when you see the routine and nothing but the routine—"

"Like, hypnotize yourself?" Purple said.

"Exactly," Miss Adams said.

"Like, say you're a monkey. Ya-eee." Everybody laughed. Miss Adams scowled. "Evangeline, take your sweater off. You make me hot just looking at you." Then she started talking about how we all thought we were reservation rats. "You think just because you're from the rez you don't count?" Everybody kind of sat back, like, *Here we go again.* The teachers were always talking about how cool it was to live on a reservation. She launched in about some native girls' basketball team from some boarding school in Montana, who, in 1904, exhibited at the World's Fair.

"They were exhibits in the fair?" Purple asked.

Miss Adams glared at her. "They had an international reputation for excellence in their sport."

Purple pursed her lips in a round little O.

"Now tell me," Miss Adams said, "what can I do to help you learn to concentrate?"

"Music," Purple said.

"No," Miss Adams said.

Then everybody else said it—"Music!"—and Purple was beaming, all pleased with herself.

Miss Adams squinted at us, shook her head, but then asked us if we promised to work, to really work, and to take ourselves seriously, to pursue excellence, and not to play the music too loudly, and not to play anything obnoxious, and we all promised everything.

The next afternoon we did our warm-up jumping jacks to the Archies' "Sugar, Sugar."

When it was time for the uneven bars, I perched like a canary on the low, waiting for Purple to come and spot me. We couldn't start without our spotters. Purple had appointed herself music monitor. She was making a big production about choosing the right record to get us swinging on the bars.

Everybody else was already into her routine—there were five sets of bars altogether, and only ten of us gymnasts. Miss Adams was always telling us how generous the BIA was to give us five sets, so that we didn't even have to share, which was another reason we should be stunning, because we got more practice time than nearly anybody else in the state.

So we each got fifteen minutes, and I was perched up there, waiting for my spotter, and she put Jimi Hendrix on the record player, and she was heading across the mat, and Miss Adams screeched, "That's obnoxious!" Purple shrugged, went back, and took Jimi off. She started sorting through the records, looking at one, checking out the back of the cover, looking at another, and so on. I was just sitting there. My turn was like half over. I looked over at Miss Adams. She was all tied up trying to get the blob, Mary Louise Enos, up and over her low bar. Purple finally found something she liked, and it was Janis Ian's "Society's Child." So she was heading toward me, and I had maybe five minutes left of my turn. Janis was singing, "Victims of society . . ." and Purple was moved to tumble. She could not contain herself. She went flipping across the mat, came out of a round-off singing with Janis, "Why can't they just let us be?"

I'm wondering if I can make her have a little accident. I wonder just how powerful I can be if I really concentrate. I close my eyes. I picture *her* falling. From some great distance. A high bar, a very high bar. I put her up there on this very high bar, and she's twirling, but her hands slip just when she's upside down, so she comes down, and there's the knee crack, the headfirst lunge toward the low, a five-inch gash across her forehead, a flip backwards, the long dive down, down, down, and *Oh, looky who's here:* me. My arms—they give under her weight, a little too much to break the fall, then jerk up hard, just enough to break the back.

I opened my eyes. I clutched my perch. A kind of lightning

was shooting through my arms. Purple was coming toward me, grinning. "My turn," she said. Sure enough, Miss Adams must've yelled, "Switch," but I didn't even hear her, and I didn't hear the end of the song, either.

Purple began chalking her hands, and I had this lightning going through my arms, like if I didn't do something about the lightning my arms would catch fire, and then I amazed myself. I swung one leg over, swung around the low bar, then again, then again, then lunged for the high. I was electrified. I bent at the hips, just like we'd been taught. Legs straight, feet overhead, I began to pump until I got a maximum swing, then rolled up and around for a perch on the high, and I didn't look at her on the mat below. She didn't have any choice. She was my spotter. She had to spot me.

I crooked my leg over the top and began to do glide kips, and I could feel the blisters building on my hands because the chalk had worn off, but I didn't care. I did three, swung my leg around, twirled once, and then let go—I leapt to the low, caught it in the crook of my knees, swung there upside down, up, almost around, not quite, swung back, reached up to hold the bar, and suddenly Miss Adams was right there watching. She said, "Karen, that's great. Good job." I huffed it back topside of the low bar. "Are you taking energy pills?" she said. I looked down at Purple. Miss Adams said, "Evangeline, take your sweater off. You make me hot just looking at you." Purple was watching me, this funny smirk on her face. I smiled at her. She smiled back.

She said, "You're hot?" She was looking at me, but she was talking to Miss Adams. Her voice was drippy sweet, as if Miss Adams's body heat was a personal tragedy for her.

Miss Adams said, "Evangeline, you stink. Take your sweater off this instant."

Purple just knelt there, her arms held ready—a good little spotter—and she was smiling, but then I saw her eyes turn cold, that hard, glittery, hateful cold, and for once, I knew that that look was not for me.

"Did you hear me?" Miss Adams said.

I knew she wouldn't tell that I stole her turn. She would never tell Miss Adams anything important.

Karen, that's great. Are you taking energy pills? I kept thinking about what Miss Adams said. I couldn't stop thinking about it. My hands were so sore! I put Vaseline on them, and the blisters soaked it right up. I was glad it was Friday. I thought maybe I could wrap them if the blisters were still bad after the weekend. I didn't want to miss my turn on Monday. *Karen, that's great,* she'd said.

She'd noticed.

Monday, guess who's Little Miss Prompt. Guess who's suited up and waiting on the bars before anybody else. She was never on time! She was always the last one to the gym because she always had to kiss Tyrone for about ten minutes after the bell rang and make him late for basketball practice. But there she was, sitting on the low bar. Looked like some kind of parrot in her sweater with those blue bloomers blousing out.

I took my time going over to spot her. I was a slow walker. She was sitting there singing, "I think we're alone, now. The beating of your heart is the only sow-ound." I didn't know how she got there so fast, had time to get the music going and everything, because they never let the Level 2s out early.

When Miss Adams yelled, "Switch," she didn't. Big surprise. I was just kneeling there, witching her—*fall, fall, fall*—but, also, I was wondering why Miss Adams didn't say anything. She was staring straight at us. She had to know that Purple was stealing my turn. She had eyes in her head.

Tuesday, I was suited up and ready to go when she walked in, prompt again. She stopped dead. From across the room, I could see her evil eyes squinting. Lightning shot through me.

All week, we played this little game. We were prompt monkeys. It was fun. It was funny. Purple's face went all twitchy when I beat her to the bars, which was three days out of five, and I was glad I didn't have a boyfriend I had to kiss.

Purple didn't like to be ignored. You could see it. I had been counting the days since Miss Adams last spoke to us: eight. I guess I had contaminated my spotter. I guess she'd turned invisible, too. By day six of her invisibility, Purple was this rabid exhibitionist, much worse than usual. Wednesday, she put on music at the beginning of class while Miss Adams was talking. Miss Adams was telling us that she had arranged for a competition with Tohatchi High School, and Purple started playing old-timey polka music, like something you'd hear at a skating rink—"Waltzing Matilda"—playing it really loud, and she was doing baby somersaults, stopping after each roll to pull her sweater down. Miss Adams didn't say a word. She just talked louder. Then Thursday, Purple talked to Lily in Navajo all through practice. Carried on this conversation at the top of her lungs while she was spotting me, which, I didn't care, but Miss Adams always cared and would send people to the office for those shenanigans. *Girls, in this school we speak English.* And her cheeks didn't get the two little red spots like they usually did when something made her mad.

Then after practice, while everybody else was showering, Purple decided to get busy. She started soaking toilet paper and throwing it on the locker room ceiling, wads of it that stuck and made a sucking sound as it hardened. When Miss Adams came in to hurry us up, she just stood there staring at the gray yuck, and then the red dots did come into her cheeks. "Who did this?" Her voice was shaky.

Nobody said anything. Purple was looking all innocent.

Miss Adams said, "Whoever did this better clean it up before she goes home today." Turned on her heel and walked out. Purple was wide-eyed and surprised.

Well, I don't know how she got in the building that night, but when I went to suit up on Friday, the entire locker room ceiling was a papier-mâché sculpture, and Miss Adams was in there studying it, her face, fire.

Purple was already dressed, sitting on the bench, rolling the tops of her socks into ankle tubes. Miss Adams said she'd like to see her in her office. Purple grinned, as if that was just what she'd been hoping for.

So we were all in the locker room. Miss Adams's office was right next to us, and you could hear everything because the wall was so thin. We were quiet because Purple was shouting, which was something I had never heard before, and I don't think, from the look on her face, Lily had either. She was shouting "You can't make me"—over and over again she said it—and at first Miss Adams wasn't shouting, but then she was: "Maybe I can't make you, but I know who can. You will not embarrass this school." We all looked at each other, because the goo was gross but not embarrassing.

Miss Adams was nowhere in sight when it was time for practice to start. Purple was sitting on the bleachers, going through records, not even trying to beat me to the bars. I went over and stood around underneath them. Halfway through the period, Miss Adams came back. She went over to talk to Betsy Cohen, then here comes Betsy with Miss Adams following. Betsy told me she was with me now.

From across the room Purple yelled, "I'm her spotter."

Miss Adams asked Betsy and me which one of us wanted to go first. Betsy shrugged. Me, I was standing there and my arms and legs felt rubbery, and my heart started thudding.

Purple was walking over, her hands in her pockets. She said it again: "I'm her spotter." Lily was just watching. Everybody was.

Miss Adams said, "Evangeline, Mr. McGilly would like to see you in his office."

Purple started chalking her hands, and she was glaring at me. She said, "I'm your spotter."

I got that thick feeling in my throat. She tucked her chin. Her eyes rolled to the top of their sockets; she was just glaring at me from under tight eyebrows. I could feel everybody's eyes, all of them, and my throat was closing. I was afraid that if I opened my mouth, vomit or something might come out. Purple, she laughed.

It was a terrible laugh.

She turned around and stomped off toward Mr. McGilly's office. After a minute, Lily went, too.

Lily came back while we were all showering. She said Mr. McGilly kicked Purple out of school, and that Purple took her sweater off and threw it at him.

I waited for her that afternoon. I sat there staring at the papier-mâché sculpture, and at her school clothes hanging on their hook. I figured she'd have to come back and get them. Sooner or later.

I didn't know what I was going to say. I wanted to tell her I can't talk in crowds. I wanted to ask her why she always had to be such a showoff. I don't know. I sat on the bench, staring at the ceiling. It was a solid wall of gunk. I looked for holes, some little spot of plaster showing through. I figured there had to be some place she missed, and I thought about how long it must've taken to cover the whole ceiling. I bet she didn't get a wink of sleep that night. I wished I had a magnifying glass so I could find that one spot she missed. When she came in I planned to say, "Hey, you missed a spot." That'd get her. I'd say, "Hey, what about this spot here?" and watch her face go all twitchy.

For a long time, I listened to the tick-tick of the locker room clock and stared at the sculpture. It looked like vomit. The whole ceiling did.

She never came.

So I'm cutting through the gym toward the door, and she's there. In the gym. The lights are off. There's just the late-afternoon sun filtering through the high, smeary windows. I see her before she sees me. I step back into the shadow of the doorway. She looks odd without her sweater, like some little girl playing at acrobatics. But she has this round ball of a belly. I'm thinking that ball's one of her jokes. Like she's tumbling with a ball under her uniform, but, too, I feel sick because it's not a ball. I know that. She takes a short run, does three front handsprings. She looks like she's been practicing for a while. I mean, she's reeling. Now she starts cartwheels. One, two, three, four wobbly, crooked-legged cartwheels. Ends with a round-off, doesn't stop—she's tossing herself every which way, and suddenly I want to scream at her: YOU DID THIS TO YOURSELF! In my head I'm screaming it.

She's just throwing herself all over that bare sticky floor, like she's trying to shake that baby out of there.

I guess there's something wrong with my eyes. I mean, all that fall I had my eye on her, watched her twirl and flip, and I never even saw the biggest thing, that belly. She didn't want me to see it, I know that. I don't even think Lily knew. It's like she pulled the shade over all of our eyes. Everybody she looked at, she probably witched: *This baby is invisible.* Except Miss Adams, who must have eyes in the back of her head.

Mama has eyes all over her head. She can see the future. She has visions. "Mark my word," she told us that next summer, "this place is going to explode."

Ronnie and Tyrone graduated in May. Tyrone enlisted in the army and went off to Vietnam. Ronnie got a one-year tuition waiver to the Colorado School of Mines. And Mama convinced Daddy to move us off the reservation, to get the little ones into Catholic schools. "Karen doesn't care where she finishes high school, do you, honey. It's six of one, half a dozen of the other to her." She figured I wasn't popular anyway. Me, I have no opinion about it.

So we moved up the Bloody Thirty to Farmington, and Daddy started to commute. Then that next fall, things on the reservation started to explode. Just like Mama'd predicted. For one, the Red Power Indians came in from the north. They took up residence inside the uranium mill. They brought rifles and guns and Daddy wasn't on shift, but Officer Chris went to investigate, and a sniper in the office shot that handsome cop dead.

Here's a funny thing. At the end of the school year, just before we moved, I was cleaning out my locker, and I found this wad of toilet paper at the bottom. It had been wet at one time and had hardened into a gray glob. I was looking at it and thinking, *How'd she get in my locker?* because I always kept it locked, but she probably had a list of every combination on every locker in school, the thug. Probably spent her spare time shopping in everybody's locker. I knew she meant it to be mean, the toilet paper rock, and I knew she thought it was funny. Ha-ha. So I tossed it on the pile of trash, but I don't know. Maybe I had a premonition. It felt weird, like heavy. I picked it back up. I was looking at it, and I saw this little bit of red in the gray. I started tearing at it, and oh, looky here. She had wrapped that ring with its red yarn, a little present in the yuck.

Maybe I should've taken it back before we moved. It would've been easy enough. Could've rolled it into the rug room when Mr. Slaugh wasn't looking, let him find it.

I like having it. I wear it around town. Here, I do nothing

but walk. I'm enjoying sidewalks. I've walked all over this town. Mama says, "Karen, try out for something." She says, "Get yourself a little after-school job."

I keep thinking I'll run into her sometime. Purple. One of these Saturdays when the Indians come to town. I'll be down at Britt Mall, or over in Brookside Park, and she'll probably have her little baby all dolled up, or maybe in a cradleboard, I don't know. She'll be toting around that baby, like she's got something, making a big deal about her little baby, and I'll say, "Cute kid," even if it's not, and she'll see this ring, and maybe she'll say, "Nice ring," or, I don't know what she'll say. Something.

When Mama saw the ring, she said, "That's pretty. Where'd you get it?"

I said, "It was a present from the trading post."

Mama curled her lip and shook her head, like she was thinking, *I'll just bet it was.* Like, *Those Mormons, they'll try anything.*

the shiprock fair

Over the bridge was the fair. Willa could hear it, and she could see it through the window. She had marched with the band over the bridge that morning, and in the Arts and Crafts tent they had hung her spider painting. Maybe they had put a ribbon on it, she didn't know.

Her father was loading bottles in the sample case, and the white man, Del Rink, was staring at her. "So this is your girl," he said.

Del Rink was her father's new boss at the water treatment plant. He was a fat man, sweet-smelling. One eye had stuck in the corner, next to his nose. Her father had not told her about that. He had not told her that Del Rink had one eye stuck in the middle of his face.

"She's a pretty girl," the white man said.

Willa stared out the window of the water treatment plant. She had helped her father test the river water since her mother died. When she was a little younger, she would ride in the cages with him to the middle of the river, and if her father let her, she would drop the bottles in the water for him. She liked to watch them sink. Her mother would wait for them on the riverbank, and she would write the reports. Her mother died from tuberculosis six years ago when Willa was eight. Since then, Willa had written the reports for her father, who could not read. Willa didn't mind writing the reports, but today, Willa had a painting in the fair, and the bluff was covered with dust from the rodeo, and she did not know why her father was taking so long, nor why she had to go in to the office with him. Willa thought of her friends walking around at the carnival, riding on the rides. She could hear the music from the rides and she could see the top of the Ferris wheel and the baskets, and she could see the banner on the bridge: SHIPROCK FAIR, 1966. It was the first time she had ever had a painting in the Arts and Crafts tent. It was one she had done over the summer. Her art teacher, Mrs. Penner, had said, "Is that a face in the web?" She had turned it so you could see the face, then turned it back so all you could see was the web. She had said, "Did you do that on purpose? Did you see one like this somewhere? Certainly," she said, "it has a chance for a ribbon."

When her father had finished loading the bottles, he began rummaging in a drawer for labels. He was looking at her funny. "This one," he said, and laughed. "This girl wants to know what happened to your eye."

Willa flushed. She could feel the white man looking at her. She stared at the floor.

"She does, does she. Well, when I was a boy, my brother stabbed me in the eye with scissors. Do you believe that?"

Willa pressed her lips together nervously and tried not to smile. Her father laughed again. Then he announced loudly, "Her name is Willa Claw."

They drove north along the east side of the river. The river was full of mud, and little islands had come up through the water. On the other side of the river pickups stood in the bushes, and people eating melons sat on hoods and tailgates. Tonight they would sleep there. They would cross the bridge and go to the fair and cross back, and they would build fires on the riverbank and cook. She had not eaten anything that day, and she was hungry.

She turned the radio on—the Navajo hour; the announcer was talking about the fair, his voice crackling from the static raised by bumps in the road, by her father racing over the dried rain welts in the dirt road. The brown case that held the sample bottles sat on the seat between them. Cotton from the trees floated on the top of the river, and cotton balls had formed in the stagnant water near the bank.

"You see his kids in school?" her father said.

"Yes." He didn't have to say whose kids. She knew he was talking about Del Rink.

"Boy and girl?"

"Yes."

"They fat like him?"

She shrugged.

"They in your grade?" her father said.

"The boy."

"Smart?"

She shrugged again.

"What's his name?"

"I don't know," she said, but then she said, "Tom."

Her father took his hand from the wheel and looked at his thumb. "Tom Thumb?" he said. He laughed without making a sound.

She looked out the window.

The cages were placed five miles apart along the river. There were three in all. They were each chained to a wooden post— tall cages, high enough for her father to stand in. Cables that served as runners stretched across the river and were hooked on each bank to metal frames. The cages looked like birdcages except that the bars were wide apart. The cables ran through a pulley wheel that was attached to the cage tops.

To ride in the cage was to have a roller-coaster ride. Once the chain was released, the cage would sail two thirds of the way across the river and then drift slowly back to the middle where the cable sagged. Her father would take the first sample from the middle of the river, then make his way back, using a black wrench that hooked to the cable, and pulling himself. He had to work quickly when using the wrench, or the cage would slide backwards to the middle of the river, and when he stopped to take his second and third samples, he had to hook the wrench behind the pulley wheels and fasten it quickly; the wrench was also the brake.

At the first stop, just outside the village, the river was wide and shallow, so they could drive right to the bank. Even in the spring at this spot, when the snowmelt was running, the sample bottles filled with mud from the river bottom. Willa's first job was to hold the cage. Now, she stood on the bank, planted her feet in the mud, and held the cage while her father unhooked the chain. She waited for him to get in and latch the door, and then she let go. The pulley wheel screamed along the cable over her head, trailed off into a thin wail, stopped finally, and squeaked back toward the middle of the river. Her father held the bars, turning his head, looking at things, and when the cage swung to a stop, he squatted and hooked a bottle to a long-handled scoop.

Willa walked back to the pickup, sat sideways with her knees sticking out, reached behind her, and turned the key one notch. Loretta Lynn was singing "I'm a Honky Tonk Girl." She looked downriver toward where the fair would be. She could see no trace of it. She would ask her father to drive to the fair when they got finished. They'd eat in the Knights of Columbus hamburger tent, and they'd throw scraps to the little red dog, the little red dog the priest owned—a dog like a rat who ran on her belly and ate the dirt off the bottom of her paws. Willa liked that dog because she was so ugly.

Her father had begun to haul his way across the cable. He would stop halfway between the middle and the bank to take the second sample, and then, near the water's edge, he would take the third. The wrench rang each time it hooked into the line, and the pulley wheels squeaked. His face strained with the effort—every muscle in his body pulled. Willa did not take after her father. Each day she looked more and more like her mother, tall and thin-faced. Her father was a small, muscular man whose body was made of rock. He looked like he had drawn his own face. He had a scar coming out the edge of his lip, curling down, and his nose was darker than the rest of his face because he'd gotten it smashed in a fight. He wore his hair in an army burr and always had. He had a stripe across the middle of his forehead from his hat, and it looked like his face began an inch below the hairline.

She could tell how close he was to the bank by his breathing. He breathed with his mouth open, a loud rasping, and the steeper the pull, the louder the rasping. When he was two pulls away from the bank, she got up to hold the cage for him.

All along the river, the cattails were splitting and their guts were trailing out. Willa tried to touch them as they drove along to the next sampling place, sticking her hand out the open window to catch the soft fuzz of the cattail innards. There had been no rain that summer. The ground had dried and split into puzzle pieces, and across the desert, dust devils rose and died. If she half closed her eyes, the river, thick with cotton, looked like snow. She had been waiting this long month for the heat to end.

She let her head hang out the window and her father's voice came whining after her. He was talking about the white man's furniture. He had watched the United van turn on the road between the water treatment plant and the Conoco, drive to the empty house back near the entrance to the drive-in, and unload waterbeds and a piano.

"He says that house is noisy," she heard her father say. Dust rolled up from under the tires; she squinted and kept her mouth closed. Her father said something that she couldn't hear because of the wind in her ears, and then he pushed her arm so she ducked back into the pickup.

"His kids join any clubs?"

"I don't know."

"His boy play sports?"

"I don't know."

"They in as many clubs as you?"

"I don't know!"

"You know anything?"

"No."

"Me neither."

She sighed. "You do, too."

"Nope," he said cheerfully. "Not me. I am empty space between the ears." She looked out the window.

They'd begun to climb the plateau and could see the Ute Mountains in the north. The river had disappeared. The river here was banked by soft pink bluffs, and the same kind of bluffs sat like isolated tables across the desert. Willa stared at the one in the east that looked like a clown's fat cheek. Here and there chrome gleamed from ruined cars that somebody had driven into the desert and abandoned.

Her father laughed suddenly, and hit the steering wheel. "He says, 'What's the crime rate like?' That's what he asked me. He said, 'Anybody breaking in to your house?' I guess he comes from Gallup. I guess he was working for the tribe over there." He poked her shoulder. "Whatsa matter?"

"Nothing."

Her father shook his head and pursed his lips. "He's a funny one. I guess he worked over there at Gallup and at Window Rock with the water treatment. I guess he's used to Indians." He laughed and poked her shoulder again. "Whatsa matter?" he said again.

"Nothing!"

He nodded and began moving his shoulders in rhythm with the music on the radio. "Fifteen years. That's what he said. Been working for the tribe fifteen some odd years."

Willa filled her cheeks with air and blew it silently through her lips. Her father put his elbow on the brown case between them and leaned toward her. "Know what else I heard?" She didn't answer him. "Know what else I heard?"

"What!"

"I heard," he said, "that they're going to close the drive-in. You know why?"

"Why?"

"Too many teenage kids sneaking in. You sneaking in?"

"No."

"I bet you are."

"Nope."

"You a little sneak?"

They would hide in the girls' bathroom when Ron Pete came with his flashlight. They would wait until dark to crawl under the fence, and then they sat on the bleachers with the walk-ins and listened to all the squeaking voices coming from the car speakers. It was funny sitting on the bleachers where the speakers didn't work, and watching the actors without voices. If there weren't many cars, they would sneak to one of the mounds, sit there, and take the speaker down so they could hear, and when they saw Ron Pete's flashlight bobbing along, they would run to the bathroom and stay in there, laughing, listening to him walking back and forth outside the door, waiting for them.

"I said, 'Put 'em in jail.' If they're sneaking in like little wild Indians."

She pressed her hand hard against her lips to keep from laughing. She wondered what Ron Pete, the drive-in cop, would think if he saw her painting in the fair. She wondered what he would think of her then. It didn't seem like she had a painting at the fair, but she did. She said, "Mrs. Penner chose my painting for the fair."

Her father played the steering wheel like it was a drum, and nodded his head. He said, "His kids in the band?"

"I guess."

"What they play?"

"She is. The girl."

"What she play?"

"Piccolo."

"Piccolo? Piccolo." He began saying the word very fast. "Piccolo piccolo piccolo." He began drumming again. "She play any solos?"

"Stop asking me! You talk too much!"

Her father stopped drumming. He looked at her, and Willa ran her tongue over her lips, tasting sand.

Her father nodded. He turned the radio off but continued nodding, and Willa stared straight ahead. She folded her hands in her lap, barely letting the fingers touch one another. She tried not to look at him, but he was doing something with his hand—he put one finger over his lips, held his chin with his thumb, pointed his finger straight, put the finger back against his lip, pointed it again. Willa looked hard toward where the river would be, toward where the next stop would be, and then she grabbed the armrest because her father had hit the gas.

They drove fast, sailing over the desert where the road had disappeared, and she held the seat to keep from hitting the roof. The road was just an impression in the dried weeds and grass. She reached over to turn the radio on, but it only coughed and sputtered. She started to turn it off, but they hit a rut, she lost her balance, and her elbow crashed into the sample case. She pressed her feet into the floor, though they came up anyway, and her knees banged together. The bottles were clinking. Maybe they were cracking and the water was spilling out. Her father shifted gears, working the clutch up and down, and she braced herself, hooking her feet under the dashboard and then grabbing the dash as her father braked at the second stop.

He opened the case, took out three sample bottles, opened his door, and started for the next cage. "Come on," he told her.

She didn't move. He stopped and turned, looking at her. "Come on!" he said gruffly.

"No."

"No?" He grinned. She lowered her head, stared out the front window, and she heard him laugh, low and dirty. After a minute she heard the weeds snapping under his feet and then the soft shush as he slid down the steep bank. She twisted the truck key, turned the radio up until she couldn't hear him anymore, and then opened her door, put the sample case on the ground, and lay on her back across the seat. Freddy Fender blasted in her ear. She thought of walking down the hall at school, arm in arm with her friends, shouting at the top of their lungs, "Mu-el Train," and of Mrs. Leitz running out of her classroom, looking like she had seen a ghost. "Clippety-clop over hill and plain, mu-el train"—and of how Mrs. Leitz had a boyfriend. David Lee gave her his ribbons. Gave her his track ribbons. Walked right up in front of everybody, said, "Here," gave that skinny white lady two blue ones and a white for the shot put, and she had turned red, and she had kept them. Willa turned the radio off. Her stomach hurt, and her throat burned.

"Hey!" he yelled. She folded her arms over her stomach and stared at the foam crumbling from the tear in the seat back. She grinned, though it wasn't funny. She put her hand over her lips and felt the wetness of her teeth and her twitching lips, which could not stop grinning. "Hey!" he yelled again. She began to pull the foam from the tear, and she thought how the truck was new last year. He didn't take care of things. He spoiled everything. He had brought it home just last summer. She listened for the chain clinking against the cage, and then sat up so she could hear better. She could hear the river slapping softly at the sand, but not the chain, and she craned her neck. She pressed her elbows to her side. A drop of sweat ran down the back of her right arm—there he went. She hadn't heard the chain, but now she heard the cage squealing along the cable, and she laughed nervously. She stood and took a few steps until she could see the top of the cage arc up toward the opposite bank, then swing back and roll to a stop in the middle of the river. She squatted. The ground below her feet was gray, fuzzy with cotton, and one sock was full of goatheads. She began picking them out. They had completely covered one sock and were sticking to the laces of the shoe. She began making a little pile of burrs.

"Hey Shik' is! Hey Shima!" he yelled.

She stared straight ahead at the Sleeping Ute Mountain and the rain clouds that had been gathering there all summer but had never come into the desert.

"Ya' at'eeh Naat'aanii. Hago!"

She put her elbows on her knees and held her face. Far to the north, the bluff tapered down, and she could see the brown ribbon of river ahead. Her legs had begun to ache, so she sat back in the dirt. She picked more cattail fluff from the cuff of her shirt, then unfolded the arm that she had been holding out the window and saw that her shirt was covered with cattail guts. It looked like a flurry of moths feeding on her.

Perhaps her mother had opened her mouth and let the moths come in. They say Willa's mother went crazy before she died, that the fever went into her head, and they say that her father had gone out and shot the ground. Over and over again, he had shot the ground, trying to wake her mother up, or because he was angry—Willa didn't know. Willa had not been angry. She had not been anything. She could not remember what she was when her mother died, though now, sometimes she missed her so much that the feeling would swim through her, and then it would be gone, like a dream.

She began to pull the cattail fluff from her arm. She was so hungry. Her stomach hurt and her head had begun to hurt. She thought of fair food, of the Knights of Columbus tent, of the potatoes frying there.

She stood and looked at the top of the cage, which had not moved from the middle of the river. She could not see him. She took a few more steps, and the cage grew as she walked. For a minute she thought the cage was empty. She could not see him. She tilted onto her toes, peered over the edge of the bluff, then squatted suddenly because he was lying there in the bottom of the cage, lying there, kicking the water, his hat over his face like a rag. What was he waiting for! For her to come? He was waiting for her to come. He would wait all day. Because he had nothing better to do. Because he was *ch'iidii*! She began to tremble. No. He was not a devil. She did not think that. He was—she did not know what he was.

She looked behind her at where the sun hung over the ship rock. It was getting late. They still had one more checkpoint, and then they must drive back. She must fill out the forms for him, and then they would go, and he would give her money. He would make her beg for money. He would say, "Two bits, four bits, six bits a dollar," and toss a quarter—because that was his joke. He would sit in the Knights of Columbus tent and he would shout it like a high school cheerleader, and

everybody would laugh because everybody liked to laugh at
him, and he would toss the quarter into the air and it would
fall in the dirt, and she would lick it up like the little red rat-
dog—

She stood. She walked quickly to the edge of the bluff.
"Hey!" he said. His hat hung over one eye only. He had been
watching for her. Now, he pushed himself up from the bottom
of the cage and sat there cross-legged. "Hey, get that for me,"
he said. He motioned with his chin, and Willa looked to
where he pointed. All along the bank there, wild asparagus
grew. She had picked it before, and cooked the tips. Now they
were grown over and flowering. They were inedible, and there
among the stalks the black wrench rested like a shadow. She
grinned. He had left it on purpose, she knew, and now he
wanted her to bring it.

"Come on!" he said, and he scrambled to his feet. "It's not
deep. Bring that to me. I'm stuck. Just take your shoes off."
He fluttered his hands. "I'm stranded," he said. "Help!" He
fluttered his hands like a little bird, took hold of the cage bars,
stuck his head through, and his hat fell into the cage. Willa
thought of her mother and how she had just opened her
mouth and let the moths come in, and then she didn't have to
worry about anything.

She began to climb down to the wrench. The sand tunneled
under her feet, and her shoes slowly filled. She did not look at
him. At the bottom of the bank she sat and pulled first one
then the other shoe off. She pulled them off slowly, held each
so the sand trailed out into little piles. She put them side by
side on the riverbank and pulled the socks off, too, leaving
each in a little ball behind the shoes. She picked the wrench up
and stepped into the water, water so warm with the sun, and
mud so soft, soft like a cow's tongue, though it gave under her
feet; she could feel little craters under her feet, and a soft flutter, as if crabs—as if ocean crabs were burrowing under. And

she stopped, just feeling the earth as it caved in, and she laughed. Her father laughed back. She held the wrench up to him. "This?" He continued to clown and prance around in the cage, and she laughed again, and then she hurled the wrench into the river away from the cage. She said, "Oops, I dropped it."

Her father stepped away from the bars. He stood in the middle of the cage, staring at her, and she stood on the bank, staring back. He was not smiling now. He had lowered his chin like a bull lowered its head. She dug her fingernails into her palms and did not take her eyes from him, and when he began to rock, when he took hold of the bars at the side of the cage, and began, at first gently, to sway back and forth, she did not flinch, and when the cage built up momentum, swinging in a wider arc up and down the river, and the wheel on the pulley began to groan, and the pulley itself stretched with the weight of the cage, when the cage began to nod left and then nod right, she laughed because he looked exactly like one of those helium-filled balloons on the Mormons' float in today's parade, the helium-filled balloons bowing to the people. He swung faster, and she laughed harder, though when the cage left the pulley, when the cable snapped and the cage ripped free, when the cable began whipping around like a live wire, and her father got the funny look on his face—for that second that he hung there in the air her father had a surprised and silly grin—then she began to scream.

The sun was setting when they drove home. They were both covered with mud. Willa was driving. Her father sat on the passenger's side, holding a wad of Kleenex to the gash in his head. His eyes were closed and he had not spoken since she pulled him from the river.

The mud coating Willa's skin made her itch, and the evening breeze coming through the window licked at the patches of skin that were not coated. She swallowed and kept swallowing. She could not get the picture out of her head. She kept seeing his face again—the moment when it disappeared under the water—and feeling his body, the way it trembled afterward.

The hand that held the Kleenex was caked with mud, and the mud made a web between her father's fingers. He had not wiped any of the mud from his face, so his skin was a deep brown clay, but there was a rim of white surrounding his lips and she thought that underneath the mud, the whole face must be that color. She concentrated on the road—she had driven the truck only twice before, on back roads like this with her father coaching—and she watched the desert swallows darting through the sky.

At the edge of the village she saw the fires on the riverbank, and she smelled the meat cooking. She looked at the river for the cage. For a while, the cage had traveled along with them, but now it was hung up in the mud somewhere.

The water treatment plant was the only building on the edge of the river. Del Rink's pickup was gone, and the plant was closed. Her father seemed to be asleep. She touched his shoulder but he did not stir. She said, "I guess your boss'll have to fix that cage." He did not stir, and he did not smile.

She would take him to the hospital. They would drive directly to the hospital, and she would park at the emergency room door—Her arms ached. The forearms ached so badly suddenly that she wanted to put them in her lap, to let go of the wheel, and her fingers on the left hand ached, too. She tried to unwrap them from the wheel. She would drive directly to the hospital, to the emergency room door.

They rounded the bend in the river, and Willa saw the lights on the Ferris wheel, a ring of white lights, and she began to hear the tin-can music. The bluffs were covered with cars and pickups whose colors had disappeared with night. High in the air above the dust, the sky was gleaming purple, and in front of her, where the road met the highway, pickups, four or five deep, blocked the road. She braked. To the left of the road was the river, and to the right was the bluff.

Her father had opened his eyes and was peering at the pickups. She turned the key off, opened her door and said, "*Shizhe'e*. Stay here." Her father dropped his hand onto his lap. The Kleenex, brown with dried blood, stuck to his forehead. "I'll be right back," she said, and she began to wind her way through the pickups toward the highway. Traffic on the highway was barely moving, and people were walking across the river walkway, and some were riding horses across. She looked at them, trying to see someone she knew. At the highway she looked back to where their truck was parked and saw her father, trailing after her, the Kleenex flowering in the middle of his face.

"*Shizhe'e*, go back!" He swayed between the pickups, walking his hands along them. She turned and hurried back.

"Go back," she told him. "Wait for me."

He grinned. She thought the dark stripes lining his teeth could be mud. "Let's go to the fair," he said.

"You're hurt!"

"Nah," he said.

"You're crazy!"

But he was leaning into her, pushing her forward. He was going to the fair. She turned and tried to hook her arm around him, but he pushed her away, so she walked ahead, turning again and again to look at him. She was trying to remember if there was a telephone anywhere over there. There would be police, and maybe an ambulance somewhere, like they had at the football games. There was always an ambulance parked at the edge of the field. There must at least be a telephone. The air smelled of animals, and the music, floating out from the rides, warbled on the wind. At the highway, she put her arm firmly around her father's waist. "Eh?" he said. "Sweetheart?" She ignored him, and he let her be his walking stick.

The highway, packed with slow-moving vehicles, was a shadow under their feet, though she kept thinking it was probably green from manure because the stink was so strong, and there had been so many horses in the parade. Her father was leaning down and looking into car windows as they walked along the edge of the road, and she saw the faces startle— white people with out-of-state plates, tourists passing through—and it made her giddy to think of what they saw: mud man with a Kleenex hanging from his forehead. It made her want to scream. White people in some cars, and Indians, none she knew—where did they all come from? Indians packed in their pickup, laughing at them—her father's body still trembled. Her father's little body. He was like a little boy, so bony and tough, and hot, hot with fever. She tried to feel his head, but he jerked away from her. "Eh?" he said. "Shi-honey?"

When they got close enough to see the people on the Ferris wheel, she led him across the highway, through the cars, and half pushed him up the low bluff. She could not see the ground because it was too dark. She knew there would be glass there. She had walked across the bridge to the rodeo many times, and she had had to sidestep the jagged glass that littered the mesa. Her father was breathing heavily, or whistling. Her father was whistling. He was whistling a single note. Over and over again, he was trying to whistle along with the songs— three or four different songs rang out from different rides. His body, so hot. She put her hand on his face before he could jerk away. The face was cold. He pushed her away again and walked away from her. They should sit down, she thought. She didn't know what it meant that his body was hot but his face was cold. They should go to the Knights of Columbus tent. They could sit there. There were chairs there, and maybe she could find a telephone. Three different notes. He was now whistling three different notes: Three blind mice. One of the songs on the air was "Three Blind Mice," and her father was whistling along with it.

In the Knights of Columbus hamburger tent, the air crackled with frying grease. The folding chairs were positioned this way and that, and the tables were smeared with ketchup and mustard. The priest and all his helpers were scurrying around with plates of hamburgers, and the little red dog was begging for scraps. "What happened to you?" the priest called, and other people called it, too, when Willa and her father walked into the light under the tent. Willa was looking for chairs, and her father was standing in the center of the tables, swaying. He removed the Kleenex from his head, stared at it in his hand, and seemed to shrink inside his skin, and she hurried to him, leading him to the chair she had found. "Coffee!" he demanded.

"Is there a phone?" she said to the priest.

"Coffee!" her father said again, and slumped down, his head wedged between his shoulders. Willa hurried to the machine, a large aluminum serve-yourself coffee machine, poured a cup, and carried it to him.

Leroy Atcitty, her father's friend, came over and stuck his hand out. Her father stared at the hand, and then touched it, said, "*Oa, Ya'at'eeh*," and closed his eyes. Mr. Atcitty sat down in a chair facing her father and spoke to him softly in Navajo. Her father shook his head and said, "This girl."

Willa, scanning the booths outside the tent for a telephone, froze.

Her father opened his eyes. "This girl," he announced to his friend, and to all the people sitting around, "clobbered me." He closed his eyes, cradled his head between his hands, and moaned. Mr. Atcitty laughed. "She reee-ly clobbered me," he called, and all around them, the people sitting in their chairs laughed. Her father shook his head and took a sip from his coffee. "Hey!" he shouted to the priest. "Bring this girl a hamburger. This is a growing girl. Bring her two hamburgers." He leaned across the table toward Mr. Atcitty and said in a hoarse stage whisper, "None for me. I'm dizzy from where she clobbered me. With her broomstick!" her father said, and the people laughed again. "That's what she clobbered me with, all right."

Willa sat down. He was all right. There was nothing wrong with him at all. He was perfectly fine, and he had tricked her again. She looked down at her hands. They looked like an old woman's hands, coated with mud and wrinkled. She scratched at the mud with a fingernail, peeling it in flakes, and then she touched her hair. Her hair was plastered with mud. She had not thought about her hair until now, and then she thought that the backs of her arms and all her clothes were also plastered with mud, and it seemed odd to her that she hadn't thought of all the places on her that were dirty.

"Not ree-ly," her father said, and tapped her on the arm. "Just kidding," he said. "Call somebody," he said gruffly. "Call a doctor," and he laughed.

She began to scrape the mud from her hair. The little red dog was following the priest around, her tiny little legs scrambling and collapsing under the weight of her body. Willa watched her bellying along, getting distracted by a scrap of food or a noise, stopping, and then twisting her head this way and that, running again and trying to catch the priest. Willa kissed the air, and the dog stopped. It looked at her, then quickly away, as if looking were a sin, and Willa kissed the air again.

Her father had begun telling the story of how he had flown through the air over the river. How it had been his first time flying because he had never been in an airplane.

She half listened, and she listened to the carnival music. "Three Blind Mice" played over and over again from the speaker in the Knights of Columbus tent. She stared out at the people walking around the carnival. Some she knew, and they ducked their heads to look at her. She didn't know what they saw.

"Ojo de Dios," the priest said. He was standing in front of their table, holding two hamburgers on one plate. The little red dog was with him, panting. Willa snapped her fingers, and the dog came over to lick them. The priest set the hamburgers down in front of her. "Ketchup?" he said. "Mustard? Ojo de Dios," he said to her father, and he leaned across the table, putting his hands on either side of her father's coffee cup, staring at the cut on his forehead. Willa scratched behind the little dog's ears, and the dog stepped on her feet, wanting more.

"Eye of God," the priest said. "Look at it," he said to Willa, and she looked at her father's forehead. There in the middle of his face was a third eye, all red and black. "Ojo de Dios," the priest said again, and wandered away.

Her father leaned over, pressing into her shoulder. She could smell the river on him. "Did you hear that?" he said. "Eye of God. Did you hear that?" He banged her elbow with his.

She looked at the meat in front of her, and she smiled. She leaned across the table toward Mr. Atcitty. "That white man at the water treatment?" she said. "He has one, too. Right in the middle of his face."

She grinned at her father, and he stared at her; he stopped laughing and stared at her coldly, and for an instant she saw him swinging again over the river, his eyes white with fury. She opened her mouth and laughed out loud.

Her father nodded. He took a sip from his coffee. He stared at the liquid in his cup, took another sip, and then put the cup down and shook his head. "This one," he said. "This one you got to watch out for." He nodded again as if he had just decided something for himself.

At her feet, the little dog was begging with pretty eyes. Willa scratched her head, tore some meat from the hamburger, tossed it in the air, and watched the fat little thing try to jump. Outside the tent, a carnival man was buckling girls in a Ferris wheel seat. He was teasing them, rocking them back and forth in their swinging chair, and they were laughing, and—

She had a painting in the fair. She remembered it now, and she felt the happiness again. Maybe it had earned a ribbon, she didn't know. She watched the carnival man pull the Ferris wheel switch and send the girls off. They rose slowly, then faster and faster, and Willa felt her stomach turn, as if she were riding, too.

blue fly

Coming home from school on a Monday morning in the spring, Sadie Evers stepped through a hole in the schoolyard fence right onto the hem of her dress. When she straightened, the left sleeve separated from its seam. Her brother, Madison, heard it rip. He turned and saw his little sister's bony shoulder naked to the world. Sadie stood trembling, her black eyes two burnt holes, the sleeve of her only school dress hanging by threads. Madison grinned.

"Now you done it," he said. He picked the ripped sleeve from her arm, then let it fall again. "You should tear the other side. Then they'll be the same."

"Be quiet," Sadie said.

"You could be a fancy woman." He leaned down, his hot breath in her ear. "You could be a bare-breasted whore."

Sadie stared, stony, at her feet.

"I saw this fancy woman once," Madison said. He put his arm around his sister and began guiding her along the path. "She took all the feeling from a man's toes. He was sitting right there on a chair in front of the Strater Hotel. She gave him a foot rub. And when she got to the toes, you know what she done? She put 'em in her mouth." Sadie squinted at her brother. "It's true," Madison said. "One by one. She put them toes in her mouth and sucked 'em, and they were dirty. But when she was done, you know what? The man starts hollering. He says, 'I cannot feel my toes, I cannot feel my toes.' He jumps up and starts waddling like a turkey. He didn't know he had any toes anymore."

Madison grinned. "That woman was a witch."

The sky was the color of Colorado columbine, and the fields were soft to the touch. All the way home, Madison told his sister about the witches and the world, but when the soddy came into view he stopped talking. The door to the shack was open, the inside, shadowy. There was no one in sight, but he could hear his sister-in-law, Katherine, talking to herself.

Madison dug his hands deep in his pockets and tucked his chin, as if against the weather. Something about the air began to feel dense. Something about it felt like pushing against water on a flooded plain.

But Katherine was not exactly talking to herself. She stood inside before the table, a leather switch in her hand, her weedy hair a tangle around her cheeks. Madison and Sadie watched from the doorway. Katherine was holding conversation with blue flies. In the shadowy room, Madison could not see her furious eyes, but her shoulders were bunched into her neck, and her hands, worrying the flies, were bone white. "Who," she was saying—then *swish*, she slapped the table, and *splat*, a fly fell—"invited you?"

The hut reeked of vinegar. A vat of brine stood sweating on the table, its sides pimpled with blue flies. In the vat was pickling beef. She had put the beef up on Friday. Or Thursday. In the dead of night, sometime between Thursday and Friday, Madison had woken to find his sister-in-law banging pots. She had woken Sadie, who sat on her cot, dog-eyed and silent, holding her quilt around her. Katherine didn't care. She had a taste for pickled beef.

The vat began to stink on Saturday, and on Sunday the flies came. Katherine was at them this morning when Madison and Sadie left, and from the looks of the winged corpses that pocked the table, she had been at them all day long.

Now, Katherine squinted past him to Sadie, a shadow in the sunlight. She raised the strap and pointed at Sadie's naked shoulder. Sadie said, "Auntie Kate, I tore—"

"Don't even," Katherine said. The strap shook in her hand.

Sadie looked at her brother. Madison watched the flies. They were the half-starved winter flies, quick but skinny. They were not the juicy, gorging summer flies, and their white guts were not visible in the mess on the table. But they were noisy, the ones on the vat and buzzing around his head, and they had been noisy all night, and all night the place had stunk of vinegar.

"You ought to take that out of here," he said.

Katherine laughed. "Ought I?" The floor, too, was a mess of flies, most dead, some walking in drunken circles.

Madison walked to the table, slapped the vat with both hands. Flies scattered, then quickly resettled. Katherine's eyes, rimmed red, were slits in her head. Madison picked the vat up. Katherine grabbed it, but Madison pulled hard, and he heard her fingernails scrape the wood, and he heard the liquid inside slosh up against the lid. Quickly, he carried the thing out of the soddy and set it down by the door of the storage shed.

Katherine didn't say anything when he came back, just watched. Her lips were thick and quivering. He watched her back, though he could hear his heart thudding. After a minute, she walked around the table. He smelled her sweat when she brushed by. She went out, and a few seconds later Madison heard the slosh of liquid. Sadie, still in the doorway, put her hand over her mouth. "She kicked it over," she whispered.

Madison shook his head and grinned. "Now we'll have bears."

"*You*," Katherine screamed from the clearing, "are *not* my children!"

Madison and Sadie stared at each other, then Sadie's eyes crossed. They burst out laughing.

Three weeks earlier, Madison's brother, Mark, had gone missing. Mark liked to go missing. Just like their old man. The old man had been gone three years now—ever since the summer of 1900. Mark usually went for a day or two, just to see the country, he always said, but when he didn't come back after a week, Katherine started fretting. She was afraid he was dead in the river. She wanted to roust all of the men in the area and make them drag the river, which Madison said was a foolish thing to do. Nobody was going to drag the river for Mark. They all knew Mark, how he was. She didn't know the people around here. Katherine wasn't from here. Mark had found her last year, up north. Last winter when the money ran out, Mark had gone up north to the high Rockies near Rico, and worked in the mines. In the spring he brought Katherine back with a wedding ring on her finger. Nobody knew if there was a paper behind the ring. If there was, Mark wasn't showing it. But she was pretty. And young. Nineteen, just five years older than Madison. Madison could see very well why Mark brought her home.

All this winter they'd lived together, the four of them, here in the soddy. "This is the foundation," Mark was always saying. "This is just the beginning." They'd moved from Durango last summer when the Ute land opened up for homesteading. They got a prime spot in the southern lowlands, just where the Rockies tapered into flatlands—good farming, good grazing. A stone's throw from the Animus River. They dug the foundation, but it snowed in August, a freak, early storm, so they laid cedar beams over the top, patched between with mud and straw. They built the roof up thick so when the wild horses came on their way to the river they wouldn't fall through; they dug a sloping channel for a doorway, and they made a thick cedar door. "Come next spring, we'll start the house," Mark said. But spring was here and Mark was not, and they were living in a hole in the ground.

The hole was dark. When the door was closed, there was no way to tell if the sun was up or down. And when they were asleep, the darkness breathed louder than they. Sometimes, in the middle of the night, Madison would wake to a clap in his ear, and he'd bolt up, his heart racing. He listened hard then for the thud of hooves overhead or for the sound of human beings, and his fingernails would itch.

In the early evening, Madison dished cold soup from the pot on the stove, a bowl for him and one for Sadie. Katherine was gone; he didn't know where. The air in the hut was still thick, and the flies were buzzing. Later, when it got chilly, he'd light the fire, but now he was hungry. "Come on and eat," he said. Sadie was sweeping. Already in her nightgown, Sadie had folded the torn dress in a neat square like a brown bread sandwich, and she had put it on Katherine's sewing basket.

Madison watched her as he ate his soup. "You think she's going to fix that? She ain't going fix it."

Sadie didn't say anything. She was doing a tour of the room, jabbing spiders in the corners with the broom, just as Katherine had shown her. "Take care of the corners," Madison said in falsetto, a sassy imitation of his sister-in-law. "The middle will take care of itself." He scuffed his shoes under the table, kicking the dead flies. "Sadie," he whined, "that's the cleanest dirt floor I ever did see."

"Shut up," Sadie said.

"She probably won't even come back. Why would she?"

"Where's she going, then?"

"Nah, she ain't coming back." He scraped his soup bowl with his spoon. From where he sat, he could see the sun perched in the lowest branches of the cottonwood just beyond the shed. He could see the pickled beef, too, where it lay in the shed's shadow. It looked like a stogie, a big stogie. Or a turd.

"She's coming back. Where's she going, then?" Sadie was sweeping the flies in a pile.

"You think she's going to sew that dress? Why should she? You think she cares if you go to school looking like a gypsy? Like a little Mexican?" Madison batted a fly. Sadie's pile looked like a little black hole on the gray floor; the floor was disappearing before his eyes. Soon it would be as dark as the pile. "You're going to school looking like a little nigger girl. I can't go with you tomorrow, honey." Madison got up. He took his bowl and put it in the bucket by the stove. The bowls from breakfast were still there, gummy with dried oatmeal. Black specks crawled in the goo. "If you go really early and sneak in and hide in the closet, maybe nobody'll notice the little ratty-tatty nigger girl, little pickaninny nigger girl—"

"Shut up."

"But I can't go with you." He walked over to the sewing basket and picked up the dress. He shook it out. He took it to the doorway, where the light was still good, and he examined the tear. He held it close to his face. "This is a big job, Sadie. Even if she comes back, which she won't, you think she wants to sit here all night in the dark—"

"Maddy, you fix it."

"Me? I ain't fixing it."

"You know how. You sewed before. Maddy—"

"I ain't no girl." He dropped the dress in a heap and stepped outside. The sun had fallen from the branches and disappeared. From here he could smell the vinegar.

"Toad," Sadie said.

Madison smiled.

"Blow up like a toad," Sadie said.

He walked over to the beef. It had rolled in the dirt and was covered in dirt; fat, dirty meat bulged around the trussing string—she'd laced it up good, Katherine had, and the string was dirt-coated, too.

"Blow up like a toad." Sadie had followed him out. She was barefoot. Her nightgown dragged on the ground. She was grinning, and her eyes were shining.

Madison shrugged. He picked the thing up by its string. It was studded in peppercorns. If he half closed his eyes, they looked like little baby flies. Sadie was screaming. She was screaming, "Blowuplikeatoad, blowuplikeatoad," and she had her hands over her ears. He tossed the thing in the air, caught it like a football, made as if to toss it to his sister, but she didn't flinch. She was coming toward him, and her hands were over her ears, and she was screaming.

"Spook," Madison said, but she was screaming. "Shut up," he said. He hurled the thing away from him, into the weeds. Then he took off running toward the river.

The hut was dark when Madison came back. He stood in the doorway. He could hear a ragged breathing, his sister's sobbing, sleeping breath. He could not hear Katherine. He stood listening for her even though he knew she wasn't there.

He brought wood in. He opened the flue, lit kindling in the stove, blew on it. The dish pail by the stove had a funny smell. In the flickering light, he could see his soup bowl. He could not see Sadie's. Sadie had not eaten. Her bowl was still full of soup there on the table. With his toe, he pushed the bucket back into the stove's shadow. He blew the twigs. They flared, and he put a log on top. Smoke and bits of fire sparked around it. He put another log on crosswise over the first, and he felt the heat wash over his wrist and arm; it was a good, satisfying heat. He wanted to curl around it. He rolled back on his heels and watched the flame eat the under-log. He imagined Katherine standing in the darkness outside, watching him watch the fire. What would she think of him if she saw him sitting calmly, his face inches from the stove?

She would think he was an idiot boy. A peanut-brained simpleton, waiting for her. That's what she'd think. Well, he was not waiting for her. He didn't care where she was. She could be dead in the river for all he cared, though he blinked quickly because the picture behind his eyes—Katherine floating in the river—made him shiver. He tossed another log in and closed the stove door.

The pail stank. It would stink more tomorrow. There was a time when washing dishes had been his job. The old man would see to it. First the old man saw to it, and when he went missing, Mark saw to it. There was a time, after his mom died and before Katherine came, when washing dishes and washing clothes and washing every damn thing was Madison's job, and if he put up a fight, if he said one little contrary word, they'd say *Blow up like a toad, blow up like a toad.*

He began to take his clothes off. He tossed them in a heap at the bottom of his cot, kicked his boots beneath, and got under his own quilt. Moonlight from the quarter moon shone through the door opening. If she didn't come soon they would have rats. River rats attracted by the heat and the stink. He wondered where she'd gone. She could've gone to the Harris's, half a mile away. But what would she say? *They are not my children.* Madison grinned in the dark. Just like a little girl, stamping and throwing a tantrum: *They are not my children.* He ought to have put his arm around her and said, "There, there, honey." He was taller than she now. Almost as tall as Mark. He ought to have put his arm around her, chucked her chin, and said . . .

He stared at the wedge of moonlight on the dirt floor.

One night last week, Katherine had undressed by the light of the stove. She had put another log on the fire, but then she left the stove door open instead of closing it like usual, and she turned toward Madison's cot. First she reached over her head. She pulled the dress up in back to undo the top buttons, then reached around from underneath for the lower ones. The dress hung loose—he had been able to see the white of her shoulders. She reached down and grabbed the skirt at its hem and pulled it over her head. She shook it once, then cocked her chin, as if listening. Her eyes were fixed on the shadow where he lay on his cot. He held very still. She draped the dress on the chair, then began to shimmy out of her shift, all the while watching him. She wore nothing under the shift. She left the shift on the floor.

Then she began to rock. Forward and backwards, heel to toe. Madison could hear air whistling through her teeth, as if she were trying not to laugh—or cry. Her body turned at an angle so that, by the firelight, he could see her breast, the nipple tilting toward the roof, and her round little belly, and her white bottom. Then she started across the room toward him, and he closed his eyes, and he closed them now, remembering.

Every bone in his body had ached with the effort to be still. He could hear the strange whistling of air through her teeth. He heard the scrape of a chair. He could not hear her bare feet on the dirt floor, but he could smell her as she neared, and he pressed into his cot. "Maddy?" she had whispered. He knew that if he were to put his hand in the air, he could have touched her. He wondered how it would have been if he had. Almost he wished he had, just to see what she would do. Mark's wife, leaning over him, whispering. "You awake?" Air hissing through her teeth; she was laughing—or sobbing. Standing over him, inches away. He felt her breath on his face. Then she said, "Fat chance." Said it loud, and he had opened his eyes, but she was walking away from him then, back toward the stove. She closed the stove door, and he listened to her get into bed.

He listened for a long time after, until he heard her breath, smooth with sleep. All that night, he kept waking, thinking she would come back. But she didn't.

Well, when they asked him why he didn't go look for her tonight, if they found her dead in the river, he would say, "She is not my wife."

He could hear a scratching in the straw roof over his head. Soon the scratching would be inside. Madison swung his feet to the floor, crossed the room to the stove, picked up the pail by its handle, put his sister's untouched soup on top of the pile, and carried the dirty dishes outside.

Something stood in the clearing. Someone. His heart started beating fast, but then he saw that it wasn't Katherine. It was Sadie. "What are you doing out here?" he said.

Sadie stood in the moonlight, staring off toward the river. "When did you go out?" He hadn't heard her or seen her. He set the pail on the dirt next to the door. She wore just her nightgown and no warm covering. Her arms were stiff at her side, as if she were a soldier standing at attention. It was a peculiar way to stand.

"You ought to come in," Madison said. "It's cold out here."

She laughed a barking laugh. Madison shivered.

The ground between where he stood and the shed was moon blue. Sadie held her feet tight together, so rigid she might have been frozen.

"What are you doing?" he whispered. She began weaving back and forth like the ticker on a clock. When had she gone out? He wondered if she was asleep, caught in a dream. "Sadie?" he said softly, but then thought he ought not wake her if she was caught in a dream. He didn't know what happened if you woke a sleepwalker. Sadie had never walked in her sleep in her whole life. He was pretty sure. It was a funny, witchy kind of a dance she was doing. It made Madison's head prickle.

He went back in. He opened the stove door, threw a log in, and left the door open, then went to his cot. He sat there, shivering. He watched his little sister's shadow bob and weave on the hut floor. She didn't come in for a long time, and when she did, she didn't get in her bed. She stood at attention in front of the stove, swaying in the firelight, her back to him, then she turned toward his cot, and he could see her face, her brows, one dark line over her eyes, her eyes, half hidden under the lids—a dreamy, spooky look on her like he had never seen before. He dug his fingernails into his palms. She took a step toward him. Then she began to take her nightgown off in the light of the fire, reaching down for the hem, pulling it over her head, slow and deliberate, just like Katherine had, and he knew that she must've been awake that night, too, and that she was awake right now. When the nightgown was a pile at her feet, when she stood naked in the firelight and he could see the little swells where her breasts were coming in and her rounding hips, her hands rigid at her sides, she said, "Maddy?" Her voice low and throaty, like a thing possessed. "You awake? Fat chance!" she shrilled. She crossed her arms over her middle and stared hard at the shadow where he sat. He shut his eyes tight.

When he opened his eyes, she was in her bed, her nightgown still piled by the stove. He got under his quilt and didn't get up to close the stove door.

Later, he startled from sleep, as if someone had clapped in his ear.

Madison awoke to the sound of his brother's and Katherine's voices outside. It was the dark of early morning. He got up and found Mark digging holes around the edge of the clearing. "Look what I brought—just guess," Mark said, and Katherine said, "Look who I found?" She'd found him on the road, coming home last night.

Mark had a two weeks' beard on his face. He had brought poplar saplings up from New Mexico. He'd been all the way to Santa Fe and had brought back a cart of saplings, and now he was planting them. He'd planted two already. One leaned south toward the river but the other stood erect, its baby branches reaching up to God. "We'll have us a natural fence, just like you wanted," he said to Katherine. Katherine stood watching, her arms clamped over her middle, pressing her lips together, but a smile kept breaking through. Mark spanked the earth near the sapling's trunk, got up, and threw his arms around Katherine, picked her up and swung her—she stiff as a sapling herself, but grinning. "You'll see," Mark sang. "I'm hungry!" he said.

"Look like finger bones to me," Sadie said. Madison jumped. She stood behind him in the doorway, a little ghost.

Mark laughed. "Sadie!"

"Like finger bones sticking out of the earth," she said.

While Katherine got breakfast, Mark dogged her, being entertaining. He told them ugly things, like about the little skinny children he saw living in railroad cars. And he told them he was going to resurrect this farm. Katherine rolled her eyes at that.

Sadie sat at the table. She was a shadow in her torn dress, her face quiet and spooked. Mark sat next to her. He said, "What's a matter with you?" He nudged her. "Want to see an angel?" He took off his hat to show his head, a little bald halo of skin in the middle of his pate. "You've got an angel for a brother," he said.

Madison laughed. He rolled his eyes at Sadie, but she wouldn't look at him. He said, "Fat chance, huh, Sadie." Sadie stared off at something past his shoulder.

Katherine put a plate of scrambled eggs in the middle of the table, and Mark reached for them. She said, "Maddy will be bald, too, don't you think?"

"Nah," Mark said. He started spooning up eggs. "Mad's got Mama's hair."

"You think?" She cocked her head and gazed at Madison. He dead-eyed her.

"Now this one," Mark said, reaching for Sadie's head and pulling her braid. "This one will be bald. She's got the old man's hair, doesn't she, Mad?" He tugged the braid again.

Sadie's chin puckered, and her eyes filled with tears.

"Hey," Mark said. "That's a funny way to laugh." Sadie dropped her head and dug her chin into her chest. "What'd I do?" Mark said.

No one spoke. Katherine stood looking at Madison, and she was smiling. She walked around the table and stood behind him. Madison sat rigidly in his chair. He could feel the heat of her at his back, and when she touched his head he flinched. She put her fingers in his hair, and she ran them over his scalp.

"Yes," she said, "Maddy will be bald." She let her fingers trail through his hair and down his neck, and she rested her hands on his shoulders. Under her hands, Madison was cold. She began to rub his shoulders. Madison glared at Mark.

"Sadie," Katherine said, "which way did you come yesterday?" Sadie studied her plate and didn't speak. Katherine was pinching him. She said, "I'll sew that dress on Saturday when I do the wash." She dug her thumbs into the soft spots between the bones, and then she put her cheek next to his. Madison could smell her. "If you came through the field, Maddy, I hold you responsible. Sadie's just a little girl."

The dawn sky was the color of gruel. Thick black clouds capped the crown of Cedar Hill, and the smell of rain was in the air. Madison was walking. Sadie was walking and running but mostly running and she was calling, "Maddy, wait," but Madison didn't wait. Madison stormed up the trail through the sage and the goatheads and the tall wild grass, and Sadie had to run with the hem of her skirt in her hands because she would surely fall and rip the dress again, and she was wet. The morning dew on the tall grass soaked her legs.

When they were just out of sight of the house, Madison stopped and turned to his little sister. "Take off your dress," he hissed.

Sadie stared at him.

"Take it off!"

From his coat pocket, he took a small cloth pouch. He opened the pouch and pulled out a spool of thread. His hands were shaking. He squatted, pulled a needle from the pouch, unwound thread from the spool, and tore it with his teeth. He began to jab the thread at the needle's eye.

Slowly, Sadie unbuttoned her dress and let it fall to her feet. She stood shivering in her shift and watched her brother sew. Because his fingers were stiff and cold and would not move, he jabbed them again and again, and when the blood came he sucked it until it was gone. The stitches were jagged, some tiny dots, some long lines. When Sadie put the dress on again the sleeve tucked a bit too far in so that the sleeve cuffed her high above the wrist, and the material bunched at her neck, giving her a little bit of a hump. She had a lopsided look to her, but she did not look like an urchin, and she smiled at what her brother had done.

All that morning Madison watched his little sister where she sat with the younger children, her sleeve a bump on her shoulder. He thought of how it used to be, before Katherine came, when they still lived in town with their old man. A lot of the time, it was just Madison and Sadie alone in the house. Mark'd go off to get money, and their dad'd go off on a drunk.

Mornings back then, the sun rose behind Sadie's eyes. She'd come to his bed and open his lids and say, "Maddy, you're hungry," and he'd say, "What time is it?" and she'd say, "Time to go huntin'." Sometimes they did. Went off hunting and didn't go to school, just the two of them.

In the afternoon, he sat half sleeping in the warm school-room. He began to play it out in his mind: how Katherine would look when they came home that day. How she would look surprised.

They took the shortcut home. Madison entertained Sadie with stories about the Mexican goatherds he'd seen down Knott's Gulch.

"You never seen one of them Mexican goats with a little puppy tied to its leg? You ever see them she-goats with their teats hanging and the little puppies jumping for 'em? The nannies can't tell a dog from a goat. What she'll do, she'll lay down when the puppy starts jumping. Right there in the sand, she'll roll over on her side and the pup'll suckle up to her, and I can't say if the dog knows she's a goat but she don't know he's a dog. She thinks she's his mama. But I'll tell you who's smart. Mexicans. You ever seen them goat-herding dogs? Mexicans sleep all day 'cuz they got experienced dogs to do their work. Goat herders suckled on their nannies' teats." Madison laughed. Every time he thought of the Mexican dirty trick on those dogs, he had to laugh, and Sadie laughed, too.

"I'll tell you something else," Madison said. "If you ever see a dappled gray like the kind they have in circuses, spit in your hand and holler, 'Good luck!' You know who told me that?"

"Mama?"

"That's right."

Sadie nodded once. Madison watched her tuck that one away in her little pea-brain. Everything Sadie knew about her mother, Madison had told her.

The morning rain had blown over and the fields steamed in

the afternoon heat. Yellow dandelions dotted the sagebrush, and the moist earth gently sucked their shoes. Maddy couldn't help but grin thinking about what Katherine would say when she saw what he had done. She'd say, "Maddy, did you do this?"

He'd say, "Yes I did."

But as they got closer to home, the back of his scalp began to prickle. He saw a thread of smoke lazing into the sky where the soddy would be. They had built the fire already. She and Mark had.

Sadie was walking ahead. Madison looked at the drunken line of stitches on her sleeve, the crooked child's seam, and the knot of material that rode her shoulder like a hump. The air began to feel thick, like water. "Wait," he whispered. "Wait!"

He grabbed her arm, began picking at the stitches he had made. Sadie tried to wrench away, but he held her hard, picking frantically at her sleeve, and the dark fury, that new look that made him shiver and was not his sister, came into her eyes. But he didn't let go. He said, "This is no good. Don't worry. This is no good." Madison picked and tore the thread until it all came loose, and the blue fly witch could not tell what he had done.

Sadie went limp, a rag doll in her brother's grasp. She stared off toward the poplars Mark had planted, which stuck like finger bones out of the earth.

where i work

It's piecework that brings in the money. You get four bucks an hour or ten cents a pocket. The old-timers can sew two pockets a minute and make eighteen an hour. They're a whiz. Most get between ten and fifteen. Me, I get four, today maybe five. This is my third day. You don't worry if you're no good at first. You catch on. You're guaranteed the four bucks no matter if you can't get one pocket on in an hour.

Sam Hunt with the measuring tape comes to my machine and measures the straightness of my stitching. He wears the tan vest, tan creased pants, brown polished shoes, white shirt. He has a perfectly formed nose, neither upturning nor down-turning, and when he stands in front of my machine, I can smell a mysterious cologne coming from him. When he comes this close, I can see that the white shirt does not stick to any part of his skin because he does not sweat.

But the fat sisters from Galveston sweat like pigs. Turn up the air conditioning! they'll yell. Today at lunch, I sat with the fatties from Galveston, Texas. You can hear them all over the lunchroom, talking about our Oregon summers, complaining about the heat and rain. They say, My bones never ached like this in Texas, and they wish they could move back there. In Galveston, the fat sisters plopped their rumps on the beach and watched the hurricanes come in. I have never seen a hurricane. When I sit with the Texans they tell me all about it.

And they say, How's your love life, darling? These women mull things over.

It is my duty to make them laugh. This is a social skill my brother, Michael, taught me. Make them laugh, he said, and you won't get fired.

Make them laugh or compliment them. Don't tell lies. Don't say things like, "I'd like to tear her little twat out"; if you have to say something like this, say it approximately, not exactly, or you'll scare people. He told me I scare people, and that's one reason why I can't hold a job—and because I tell lies. If you have to tell lies, tell little ones, he says. Try not to talk out loud when you're not talking to anybody.

At lunch yesterday, when they asked me about my lover, I said, He has a waterbed on his roof.

A waterbed on his roof? they said. In this rain?

Some laughed, some didn't. It's difficult to say what will make the women around here laugh.

But I admire their industry. They hardly make mistakes. Sam Hunt docks you a pocket for every mistake, and these add up.

Sam Hunt drives a scooter to work, a very little one. I have seen him from the bus window. He drives on the edge of the road, on the white line, and the Sandy Street bus could squash him like a penny. Then who would see to the timecards? It takes a certain kind of man. Serious. Not a drinker, I'd say. Nice-fitting suit, gleaming face.

My brother says my face is better than what you usually see. I would marry my brother in an instant, though he's sinister and disrespectful.

Michael drives a taxi and knows the timing of the traffic lights by heart. He drives two fingered, with his foot both on and off the gas pedal, never speeding up, never slowing down, through the city neighborhoods. Some nights I sit on the passenger's side and the customers sit in the back. My brother's taxi smells like fire. Cinder and ash. In the ashtrays, fat men have stuffed cigars.

I wouldn't mind a fat man. A fat man would be somebody you could wrap yourself around and never meet yourself coming or going. If I married a fat man, I'd draw stars on his back every night. I'd say, How many points does this star have? Now pay attention, termite, I'd say. How many points does this star have?

In his taxi, my brother totes around the downtown whores. Some have the names of the months. June, July, and August. Ask them how much they make a night. Depends on how fast your brother drives, they say. Hurry up, baby, time's money, they like to say. And they spend it in Riverside Park, just junkies in Riverside Park.

It smells like garbage under the bridges in Riverside Park, and those houses over there? In the housing projects, don't go up to a black woman's door. They don't want you. Don't go up to the men on the steps. Keep your hands at your sides. Walk fast or run. Don't look in the windows of a car slowing down. Walk slow if there're dogs or they'll chase you. Keep your hand on your purse. If somebody approaches you, if he gets within ten feet, say, I am fully proficient in the use of semiautomatic weapons. My brother bought me a gun when I moved out on my own, because a woman living alone in this city should be able to defend herself. You go for the knees. We put cardboard circles on a fence post in the country. I can hit them a majority of the time. If you go for the heart or head and murder a person, you could be held liable by the dead man's family, even if he broke into your apartment. This is the justice system in our country, my brother says, and he's right. The justice system in this country treats us like a bunch of stinking fish.

There. A perfect pocket. This is a keeper, so that's one. These are my practice days. They give you a couple of practice days to start out, and after the third day or so you begin to develop a system. Like, one thing is not to stop when you're coming to a corner—not to slow down or speed up and keep your hands going with your foot on the pedal, and just turn the corner without thinking. If you ruin one, put it in your purse—if it's really bad.

Next week we're moving to a new line. Sam Hunt said when he orientated me that we're moving out of the blue and into the white. We'll have enough blue by the end of the week. How's your eyes? he says. The white stitches on the white material can blind you, so remember to blink often.

There's something wrong with my eyes. I can't cry. I'm just a happy idiot, my brother says, but I say there's something wrong with my eyes. They are deteriorating in my head. I have that condition—you read about it, where the eyes dry out unnaturally. I don't cry.

All of the women at this table wear glasses. And smoke. The lunchroom's like a chimney. And they say, How's your love life, darling?

The reason I'm not married yet is because I haven't found the right man. I don't know who he is, but I'll know him when I see him, and he'll look like something, and he won't whore around. Which, I'd shoot him, any man who whored around on me. Like that man in the laundry room. He was married because I saw the ring. And he says, How thin are your wrists? Look at how thin your wrists are. See, he says, I can put my fingers around you and not touch any part. A married man said this.

A lot of the good ones are married. He had green eyes and a friendly manner, and he asked me which was my apartment. He lives right above me—him and his wife. Says, Come up and watch TV sometime. I may just do that. I would like to see their home and their furnishings.

I will ask him to help me move furniture in. When I get my first check I'm going to buy a lamp, a nice brass one, and when I save enough I'm going to buy a brass bed, too, and one of those checkerboard coffee tables, the kind with different colors of wood in squares, and some rugs, throw rugs, and ask them to dinner, the man and his wife, which, you could never ask anybody to dinner at Michael's house because nobody ever does the dishes, and there's nothing in that house but Bob Marley posters and dirt and screaming fits.

My brother has paid my rent for the last time. If he's got to have such a screaming fit about it.

Outside the window in my new apartment on the east side is a mystery tree. We don't know what it is. I've asked around but nobody knows. On a muggy night if you don't turn the light on, you can see animals in the tree. Opossum. Eight, nine, ten of them, gliding along the mystery tree and the tree's branches all in a panic. Black like tar, the branches gleam in the moonlight, all the little opossum claws scratching where you can't see or hear. Shall I open the window? my brother said when he came over. Want some pets? Hold on to your hair. They could get into your hair. He says they're rats, but I have seen them up close. On this, he's wrong. He says this because he's jealous.

Who pays your rent? he says. He says, Who the fuck pays your rent?

My brother has paid my rent for the last time if it's such a big deal.

"My brother had a fire in his taxi."

"What?"

"My brother drives a taxi and somebody started a fire in the back seat."

"Ain't that something." She's the nice one. She says, Sit with us, honey, and tells me about the Texas hurricanes. She's someone you can talk to. "Did he have insurance?"

"What's the difference between a tornado and a hurricane?" The woman has bitten her fingernails to the quick. You can see it from here.

"A tornado? You know, I never considered it. Hey, Lynn. What's the difference between a hurricane and a tornado?"

"One's by sea, one's by land."

"One thing I do know. They can both come up on you in a minute."

"Same with a fire. My brother had a fire in his taxi."

"Ain't that something."

"Somebody left a cigar or cigarette burning in the back. It went, just like that."

"Anybody hurt?"

"They're made of straw. That's why the seats can go just like that."

Then you're walking.

So let him walk. See how that feels.

In the projects a man came up to me. He said, Woman? Woman? He said, Where can I find a pepper grinder? He said for fish, that he was cooking fish and he wanted some fresh ground pepper, and then started laughing and laughed his fool head off.

In the projects, you can get shot and nobody's going to look for you. In the projects, someone has busted out every street-light, and there's glass in the street, and children playing in it. In the projects, you can walk down one street, up another, a street without lights so you don't see the dirty yellow walls all alike, street after street, with dogs that'll chase you and black women who don't want you, and it smells like garbage in the projects. Those people are filthy.

I don't care if it is cheaper there. He says, You don't have to worry. I'm not going to let anything happen to you. Don't make me cry, Michael. Joyce, I'm not going to let anything happen to you, he says. I told him I'd cry, but there's something wrong with my eyes.

Damn! Now that thread's broken. Where's Sam Hunt? Where's that weasel? Run the flag. Got a problem, he says. Pull this little string. I'll see your flag and respond. They can't be having girls run up and down the aisles looking for the weasel. That way if anything's missing or disturbed anyplace in the vicinity, we'll blame it on Betsy Ross's ghost, he says to me. He has equipped every sewing machine in the place with a little flag. If you have to go to the bathroom, raise the flag, take your purse, don't put it on the floor in the stall because the weasel is not responsible for stolen or lost property.

Somebody should burn that man up.

There are instances where fires occur by spontaneous combustion, and instances where water will not put a fire out. There are oil slicks on the ocean. In dreams, too—there are people burning on the ocean or in impossible places, instances where burning oil floats on water and your clothes are on fire, and your hair is on fire, and in the water the fire goes inward. If it's dirty with oil and muck. Sometimes there's no way to put the fire out.

In such a dream, go into a well. Make it from rocks. The bottom of the well is very smooth, and the rocks are cool. Close your eyes. Put your cheek against a rock. If you're dizzy, reach your arm out. Touch the other side. Twirl in a circle. Put yourself in a blue well, and keep your eyes closed. Turn around and around until the fire stops.

• • •

"Joyce? What is it?"

"My thread broke."

"Your thread broke? Do you remember how I showed you to reload your thread? Did you try that? Here. Show me. Remember? Here, now, you hook it around this wire first. Remember. Okay, good. That's right. Yes. Down the pole, into the needle. You pull that back or it's going to knot when you begin to sew. Good. Very good. See? That wasn't so hard. Was it?

"How you doing? You getting along okay? You getting to know people?"

"Yes."

"Let's see what you've done today. No, now you're holding your material too tightly. That's what'll give you the tangled stitches. Remember how I told you to roll it under the foot—just like it's a rolling pin and you're making pie crusts. Remember? You bake, Joyce? Just roll it under the foot with a nice, steady movement."

"Yes, I bake."

"No, now this one's not going to work. See, you've got the X in the corner. You can't overshoot the pattern or you'll have a little X. See? And here's another one.

"Joyce, where are the rest of them? I counted sixty pockets out for you this morning. Now I count—let's see . . . Where're the rest of them?"

"That's all you gave me."

"No. This morning I counted out sixty, and now there are . . . They can't just disappear. Let's see. Forty-eight—

"This is your third day? You're not picking this up, are you? Maybe we should transfer you to pant legs. There aren't as many angles. Come and talk to me when your shift's over."

"I can't. I'll miss my bus."

"Catch the next bus. Come and talk to me. We'll take a look at your file. See what we can do."

I can do this.

This is a cinch. Go forward and backwards to lock in the stitch. Be careful not to overshoot the pattern—be careful not to overshoot the pattern because that's when the X occurs. You can't rip it out because the buying customer will see where the ripping occurred. Now that's ruined. Put it in your purse.

Here's the rest of them. These are ruined. I forgot about these in my purse.

Forgetting is not lying. I'll say, I didn't lie. I forgot, and that's the truth.

What's she smiling at? What's so funny about that pocket? That's a hilarious pocket. These women will laugh behind your back. They listen in on every conversation and then they laugh behind your back. Well, fuck them.

I can do this. So, let them laugh. You go forward and backwards. Every system has its routine. In a house when you live alone, you check the rock by the front door when you come home to see if it's been moved in your absence. If it's been moved, someone has gone in your house. This is just real funny. I'd like to squash her pea-brain. Now that's ruined.

Check the rock and you check for broken windows before you unlock the door, and you keep your gun in the drawer by your bed. I'm going to tell him to give me another chance. This wasn't so good today, but tomorrow's a different story. My brain's ruined for this day. That's a sad thing how a woman will just laugh in your face like that. They think they're so hot.

You keep your gun in the drawer by your bed. If, at three in the morning some person breaks in your house, you take the phone off the hook, dial 0. You don't have time to dial 911. You've got your gun and you're kneeling in bed or on the floor, and you say, I'm fully proficient in the use of semiautomatic weapons. I live at one-one-three-four East Holly. You're saying this to the operator who will call the cops.

Say, "I am fully proficient in the use of semiautomatic weapons—"

"What?"

"What are you looking at?"

"What did you say?"

"I didn't say anything."

"Yes, you did."

"What are you looking at?"

"Hey, don't worry about it. Don't sweat it. Sam's okay. Gets a bee in his lugudimous maximus every now and again, but he's okay."

"They're going to fire me from this job."

"Nah, they ain't going to fire you."

"He's going to look at my file."

"Listen—"

"They look at your file, and then they look at you."

"You've got to—"

"Don't look at me."

"Now, honey—"

"Don't look at me! Don't look in my face."

Don't look anywhere.

They open your file and then they fire you. Everything is ruined now. So who cares.

These are ruined. I've ruined these. Meaning to or not doesn't count. Did you or didn't you? Did you or didn't you? he'll say. He'll call me on the phone. Did you or did you not? Michael will say. I'll say—

When Michael calls—

I'll say, I didn't get to these yet. These were misplaced. I'll say. I'll say, I forgot about these in my purse.

This place is filthy. Somebody ought to clean this place up.

You just do your work. You just pay attention.

I'll leave my coat in the locker. I'll sneak out the back way, and I'll leave my coat in the locker.

I'll say, These are my practice days, Mr. Hunt. I can do this.

I'll sneak out the back way.

I'll catch the Sandy Street bus. If I miss the Sandy Street, I'll catch the Burnside. I won't look at the bums sleeping there. When I walk across the bridge, across the Burnside Bridge—if they ask me for money, I'll look straight ahead.

When Michael calls to ask me how it went—if my brother calls—

I'll say, Not too bad. That's what I'll say.

He'll say, Way to go, Joyce. That's money in the bank.

For dinner, I'll make mashed potatoes or I'll make rice. I'll sit at the table by the kitchen window. I'll watch the sun go down.

I will set my alarm for six so I can catch the Sandy Street bus at seven because the Burnside bus will get me here too late. Sam Hunt sees to the timecards. Don't be late or you're docked pockets, and these add up.

I will set the alarm for six and I'll go to bed at ten. If I wake up in the night—if a dream or nightmare wakes me . . . I must not wake up in the night. A working girl needs her sleep.

crazy yellow

Pete Lochte lay on his mother's bed watching a wad of aluminum foil. The wad didn't move. He'd stuffed it under the sliding door that separated the kitchen from the bedroom. Mice lived behind the wall. They hadn't checked the stove before they moved into this place, but if they had they would have found a tray of droppings. When they did, they stuffed every hole in the apartment with newspaper. Then last Sunday morning Pete watched a mouse tear newspaper piece by piece out of the hole under the kitchen door. Once the mouse crawled in the hole, Pete stuffed it with aluminum foil, a tightly wadded silver bomb that no mouse could possibly break through. Still, he watched the bomb every day, just in case. So far it hadn't moved a bit.

He got up and walked over to the foil. His mother said that by now the mice would be carpet behind the wall, that they all must have died, but there was no funny smell. He reached down to touch the bomb, wiggled it like a loose tooth, was wiggling it when the phone rang.

"Hi, sweetie." He could hear traffic behind his mother's voice. "How's everything?"

"Where are you?"

"I'm still in Portland," his mom said. "Hamburgers tonight. You and Lynn are going out. How about that?"

Pete didn't say anything.

"Peter," she said, "the doctor wants to keep me overnight for some tests. Honey? It's nothing serious. Just some tests."

She must be in a phone booth. He could hear voices behind hers.

"Let me talk to Lynn," she said.

"She's not here." He could hear horns blast.

"Where is she?"

Pete had spent the afternoon on the beach with his aunt Lynn. She lived in Tillamook, just five miles down the road, and she would drive over when his mom had to go to Portland. But today when they returned to the apartment and found his mom still not home, Lynn had to leave.

"She went to work."

His mom was silent. Finally she said, "She just left you there?" She told him to call Lynn at work, to tell her to come and get him, but then she changed her mind and said she was coming home, that she'd tell the doctor they'd do it another time.

"I'll call her," Pete said. "It's okay."

She was quiet for a long time. Finally she told him that he should call Aunt Lynn right now, and that she'd call back in ten minutes. "And Peter," she said, "it's nothing serious. Just some tests."

"I know."

Pete put the receiver back in its holder. He picked up the phone book, flipped to the back where his mom had penciled Lynn's work number. She'd have to wear a hospital gown since she didn't have any clothes with her. She'd have to wear one of those things that tied in the back, and if you walked around everybody could see your naked backside.

The first time she was in the hospital his dad took him to visit, and they saw a woman walk down the hall in one of those things. His dad said, "Now that's a vision." That was three years ago. Pete hadn't seen his father in nearly six months. He was working in Alaska on a fishing boat.

Pete picked up the receiver and dialed 3-4-7—but then stopped. He would be nine in two months. He put the receiver back down.

He went into the bathroom and looked at himself in the mirror. He made his right eyebrow go up and his nostrils flare. His mom teased him when he made faces in the mirror. "Are you handsome?" she'd ask him. "How handsome are you?"

He curled his lip and made his monster face. He thought about the sleeping bag in the empty apartment downstairs. She didn't know a thing about that. There were lots of things about this place that she didn't know. He'd seen the rolled-up bag through the porch window yesterday, and he walked around the house and found a broken window in the back. In the woods once, farther down the beach, he stood shadowed by trees and watched a man and girl hammer out the glass from one of the rentals, then slide into the house. A few days later he watched a man in a suit and a uniformed cop pick the glass from the sand, hold it in their hands, and stare at the hole in the window. He didn't tell them about the man and the girl, though, and he hadn't told his mom about the sleeping bag downstairs because he liked being the only one who knew.

The phone rang, and he ran back into the bedroom.

"Is she coming?"

"Yes."

"She got off work?"

"She's coming."

"Good. I'll be home early tomorrow," his mom said. "Tell

Lynn I'll pay her back. Tell her you can eat whatever you want, that I said so."

If he had money, he'd walk to Quik Stop and buy something to eat. There was nothing to eat in this house. Just mochi and miso and seaweed in the cupboards, carrots and wheat grass in the refrigerator. His mom said brown rice and carrots were the perfect foods, that they brought balance and harmony to the body. When she first got sick, she threw out everything good to eat in the place and stocked up on mochi and seaweed. She told Pete and his dad that these things would taste good, too, once they developed their taste buds. Pete and his dad used to sneak out when his mom was napping. His dad would whisper, "Let's get some dogs." Then they went to Quik Stop and stuffed themselves on hot dogs.

Pete stared at the bomb. It did not move. He wondered where there would be money. They kept a junk drawer in the kitchen. Pete opened it, started pulling out shoestrings, a leather glove, clothespins, cards, screws. He dropped these on the floor and dropped batteries, matches, incense sticks. He found a quarter, three pennies, a Chinese coin with a square cut out of the middle. When his mom was sad, she liked to take Chinese coins and get out her *I-Ching*. "Whatever's happening inside you, remember that you're about to change. If you feel like you're in a well, you're about to climb out of it. That's the nature of life." His dad used to roll his eyes when she threw the coins and read from the *I-Ching*. He called it her hocus-pocus book.

Pete put the coins in his pocket. He walked into the bedroom jingling the change in his pocket, and he picked up his mom's black purse. He found three dimes and a penny in a zippered pouch. He found tissues in the purse and mints, five pens, and an old picture of his dad. His dad's green eyes were half closed, and his lips shone. His lazy brown hair hugged his head. He looked ready. "We're ready, aren't we, Pete?" he liked to say, and they'd put on their jean jackets. They were ready for anything. Pete released the picture and watched it float to the floor.

His mom kept many vitamin jars on the bottom nightstand shelf, jars filled with acrylic paint, plus two with rubber bands and two holding paintbrushes. He emptied the rubber bands and the paintbrushes but saw no coins. He picked up one of the paint jars, unscrewed the lid, brought the open jar to his nose, and sniffed. The jar was brown. The room was dusk. It was impossible to see the paint's color, so he picked up a brush, dipped it in the paint. White. It dripped into the vitamin jar and over the lip onto the side, running down to Pete's finger. He held the brush like a dart and torpedoed the aluminum foil bomb. White paint streaked the white wall and the wood floor. "Right on," he said.

He put the open jar on the floor and took another. He un-screwed the lid, sniffed. He took another brush from the floor, dipped. It came out globbed yellow. "Crazy yellow." He bombed the aluminum, hitting it square. It looked good. Even in this darkening room he could see that yellow aluminum, and it looked good. He got off the bed, taking the yellow paint with him. He picked up the brush, lay on his stomach, dipped the brush in the paint, and began to coat the bomb. He painted carefully, digging with the bristles into each wrinkle, painting section by section.

He decided to paint the bomb on the mouse's side, too. He pulled the wad from the hole, smearing yellow on his fingers, and painted wrinkle by wrinkle, double coating it so that when he stuck it back in the hole, yellow oozed around the edges like egg yolks. He was hungry!

He dropped the brush and got up, walked to the portable

wardrobe case and threw open the doors. Most of the clothes were his mom's. He began going through her coat pockets: raincoat, car coat, cashmere coat his dad bought her. Her city coat. Before she got sick, they used to go to Portland on dates, all three of them, and his mom wore the clothes his dad was always buying. Nasty clothes, she called them. Stockings with seams up the back and skinny dresses, a black one and a red one and a shiny blue one. All through the date his dad would say, "Doesn't our girl look great? Isn't she something?" They went to movies or to the Rose Garden, and before they came home, they always went to the deli for seven-layer chocolate fudge cake.

Pete stepped closer and put his face in the coats. He couldn't remember what seven-layer fudge chocolate cake tasted like. These clothes smelled like his mom. His robe had fallen to the floor. He didn't pick it up and hang it next to hers on the door. She should have taken her robe to the hospital so she wouldn't have to wear one of theirs.

Well, she couldn't have. She hadn't known she was going to the hospital.

Pete backed out of the closet and sat on the edge of the bed. The new lumps were no larger than ants, Lynn had told him today. Smaller than the first time. Just little brown sugar ants you could smash between your fingers.

The arm from a white shirt in the closet stuck out, handless but stiff. Yellow streaked the cuff. Pete looked at the paint on his hands. He walked back to the closet and rubbed the cuff, but more paint smeared on from his hands, and now he noticed that there was yellow paint on the cashmere coat and on a gray turtleneck, and—there was yellow paint on everything he had touched. He wiped his hands on his jeans, then put them behind him. He walked into the bathroom and turned the light on. When he looked in the mirror, he saw a little yellow mustache above his lip, and when he took a towel and rubbed it, the mustache stayed but his face where he rubbed turned red, and when he soaped it and his hands, turning the water on as hot as he could stand, his hands and face turned very red but the yellow stayed. He shoved the towel in the hot water, turned the faucet off and took the dripping towel into the bedroom. He rubbed the cuff with the towel as hard as he could. The wetness made the paint look green, but it didn't make it go away. He wedged himself between coats, dropped the towel, and scraped the cashmere with his fingernail, but the paint smeared then, and he remembered it took a long time for this kind of paint to dry, how his mom always said, "Don't touch the paint," when she finished a canvas because it took so long to dry—Pete pushed the clothes as far apart as his arms would stretch. He backed out and sat on the bed.

The phone began to ring. He stared at it. On the third ring the answering machine clicked on and he heard his mother's voice saying they weren't home, please leave a message, and then he heard her: "Hey, you guys, are you there? I bet you're at dinner. I bet you're eating something trashy," she sang, and Pete hated it, suddenly, the singsongy tone she sometimes used when she talked to him, as if he were a child. As if he were two. He stared at his own fat cheeks in his mom's *Paradise* painting on the wall. His three-year-old self with its fat cheeks, his little smiling self, and his little crying self, and his little sleeping self—all the angels in this painting had his face, though his mother had changed the hair color. And the elf on the horse in the painting next to *Paradise* had his face. His four-year-old face. She had made his hair golden and his eyes green. And in the next painting, the little prince had his five-year-old face.

This room smelled. It smelled like paint. "I'll try back in a few hours," his mom was saying. Pete pushed himself off the bed, banging his arm on the bedpost. He headed for the stairs. He could not stand this place.

Through the screen on the porch door he could see a man sitting on the step. There was a small, smoking grill on the ground. The grill had only two legs. The man had propped the third side up on rocks. Pete had seen a broken grill just like it farther down the beach.

This man was completely bald and wore a dirty white T-shirt and jeans. He was drinking a beer. Beside him a fish—wide, flat, swollen-lipped—leaked onto a paper bag. There was a section of newspaper next to the fish, and the man kept leaning over and peering at it. Now he picked the paper up, brought it close to his face. Before Pete could think, the man was standing and coming toward him across the porch.

"Well, hello." He grinned. A tooth was missing on the top. "Is there a porch light in there?" Pete flipped the switch. "I'm your new neighbor. Charlie Alexander." He motioned toward the empty apartment with his thumb. "Just moved in." Pete didn't say anything. The man peered through the screen. "And who are you again?" He poked his tongue through the gap where the tooth should've been, and looked Pete up and down. "Cat got your tongue?"

After a minute, the man shrugged, turned, and walked back to the porch step. He sat half-turned so Pete could see the side of his face. He held the newspaper close to his face, studying it.

Pete opened the door and stood leaning against the door frame.

"Know what it says here?" this Charlie Alexander said. His skin puffed and folded around his eyes like an old man's, but the rest of him didn't look old. "It says, 'Ruling a large kingdom is like cooking a small fish.' Now what do you suppose that means?" The man poked the fish. "Would you say this is a large fish or a small? I mean for cooking."

"Where'd you get it?"

The man smiled. He crumpled the beer can and threw it on the ground with two others. "Caught it off the rocks." He pulled another from its ring in the six-pack. "You ever seen one of these? These are lucky fish. Sunfish."

"If you found it dead on the beach, you shouldn't eat it."

The man took a drink, watching Pete. He put the can beside the fish. "No?"

"A bad taste to her," Pete said. Last week he and his mom were walking on the beach and saw a man pull in a fish that looked like a perch, though it wasn't, and from its stomach, little fish dripped out, dozens of tiny little fish the color of nothing. It lay there in the sand, and it didn't flip because it was dead already. "She's no good now," the fisherman had said. "A bad taste to her." He told them to take the babies to the water because they had a chance, so Pete and his mom scooped them up and ran to the water with them.

"Well," Charlie Alexander said. "And who are you again?"

Pete didn't answer. He walked to the porch railing, threw one leg over, mounting it. There was a spot of yellow on his tan shorts, almost invisible, almost the color of the shorts. Pete put his hand over it, but the spot was wet. He rubbed the wet fingers on his blue shirt. He couldn't see the yellow on the blue, not really. Just a bare streak of yellow that looked green.

He didn't know how Charlie Alexander, this Charlie, got here. There was no car parked in the dirt drive nor under the trees out back. In the weird porch light Charlie's tanned face was the color of mustard. Pete thought about how he'd run out toward the water if the man pulled anything. Pete could feel live fish flipping in his palms. Right now he could feel them.

Charlie stood, walked down to the grill, and put his hand over it. He had used driftwood instead of coals for the fire. He walked back to the porch, picked up the fish by its tail, and flipped it onto the grill, and it sizzled. "First time out, I catch me a damn sunfish." He wore a knife in a belt holder, and now he took it out, opened the blade, sat on the step, and began shaving his thumbnail. "One problem with me?" he said. "I got no feeling in my extremities. So you tell me if I'm bleeding." He held his thumb out to Pete and Pete jerked back. The man laughed. "You're white, boy. Did I scare you?"

"No."

"White as an albino coyote." He slid his knife under the fish, lifted the tail, and looked at its underside. The fish began to drip onto the coals, and flames shot up through the grill, licking around the fish's sides. The man didn't wear shoes. He squatted, balanced on his toes, and Pete could see that his heels were cracked, the cracks filled with sand. His legs didn't shake. Pete had tried to do yoga with his mother, and they sometimes squatted in that kind of half-squat, but they couldn't do it for long because their legs shook. This was a strong man.

He flipped the fish over. The tail was black but most of the fish was rosy brown, and there were stripes from the grill. He blew on his fingers and grinned. "Am I burning?" he said. "You've got to tell me if I'm burning because I got no feeling in my extremities."

"Why not?" Pete said.

"Frostbite. Got it up in Canada a few years back, which is how I lost my toe." He held out his left foot. There was a bony stump where the toe should've been. "Lost my toe and all feeling in my fingertips, which should make me a good cotton picker, don't you think?" He laughed, his mouth wide open.

He asked Pete if he'd ever been camping, and Pete said sure. "I mean real wilderness camping." He looked Pete up

and down. "Up to Canada they got whole packs of these albino coyotes. You ever seen one of those?"

"No."

"You probably don't have the eye," Charlie said. "They're
all over the place but most people can't see 'em."

The fish on the grill hissed and flames leapt all around it.
"Come here, hold this bag for me, will you? Come on, I won't
bite." He slipped the knife under the fish and started lifting it
from the grill.

"Once," he said, "I'm driving, this was on an Indian reservation over in Arizona. Pick up the bag and hold it real close.
That's it. Fish'll fall apart, we don't watch out." Pete got the
paper bag and the man slid the fish onto it. The bag felt heavy
and warm. "You eaten? You're welcome," he said.

He sat back on the porch. "Yeah, so it's dark. Come on," the
man growled when Pete didn't sit. "You scared of me?" Pete
shrugged. He sat down to show Charlie he wasn't scared of
him. Charlie took his dirty knife, wiped the blade on his jeans,
held the fish by the gills and sliced from neck to tail. Pete
wondered if a fish dead off the beach would smell this good.
He didn't think so. Charlie took hold of the tail and began
loosening the bones from the flesh. "I'm driving along, and I
see this white dog running on the side of the road. That's what
I think at first, but then I notice how it's running. It's running
toward me, but this dog isn't spooked by my lights, and it
knows where it's going. You ever seen a coyote hunt? Smart
animals. They're pack animals. They'll corner a deer, deer or
antelope, surround her, back her into a canyon, and then just
sit there and howl. Paralyzes the prey." The man put the
bones on the edge of the porch. "I mean, the coyotes take
their time, and when the prey's paralyzed with fear—" He cut
into the fish, spearing a chunk, holding it on the tip of his
knife to Pete's mouth. Pete jerked back. Charlie laughed. Pete
opened his mouth and took the fish. He held it in his mouth,

tasting it. It tasted good, and he bit into it, letting the juice run over his teeth and down his throat. Charlie speared a chunk for himself and swallowed it with beer. "So anyway, this white animal is running toward me like he owns the highway, and I say to myself, I say, 'Charlie, slow down.' Because see, it's a coyote, but no ordinary coyote. I got the eye." He touched the skin near his eye with the knife point. "Five miles down the road, you know what?"

"What?" Pete took more fish that Charlie held out to him.

"I come on an accident. A real bad one. Somebody died, that bad. I'm the first car there. And you know what?"

"What?"

"If I hadn't slowed down it would've been me in that accident. What do you think of that?"

"You were lucky."

"No luck about it. The albino coyote warned me. But you gotta be able to see 'em. Most people can't."

Pete picked a chunk of fish from the paper with his fingers and ate it. His stomach wanted more and so did his mouth. He ate chunk after chunk and so did Charlie Alexander. The fish was better than good, like it always was when you cooked it on a grill. He and his dad had cooked fish and deer and rabbit on spits over campfires lots of times.

Far away where the sun had gone down, the ocean gleamed like a dime or a spaceship. A tiny little one-man spaceship. Sometimes when he woke in the middle of the night he thought of what it would be like if spacemen did come and choose a special few, and if he was one of the chosen. He could put himself to sleep thinking of what it would be like on an alien spaceship.

Down the beach somebody had made a campfire and people walked around it, just dark shadows, five or six people, probably roasting wieners. "You know what? You know what somebody did in this apartment?" Pete said.

"What?"

"Built a fire. Somebody went in there and built a campfire in the middle of the floor."

"No," the man said.

"Yes, they did. They put a rug over it, but if you move the rug you can see where they built it."

"How do you know?"

"I saw it. I'm telling you. You can look. There's no hole but the wood floor's all burned in this one place."

"And what were you doing in there?"

Pete looked off down toward the people.

"I bet I know who did it. I bet it was you."

"No, sir."

He pushed Pete in the side of the head. "I'll just bet it was you," he said, and Pete grinned, though he hadn't done it.

"No, sir," he said again, but he couldn't stop grinning.

"Smiley," the man said. "That your name? Smiley McGee?" He laughed. "Smiley, Smiley, Smiley McGee." He pushed Pete in the shoulder, pushed him hard, and Pete lost his balance. He caught himself with his hand, and the man pushed him again, and he was laughing—Pete could see the roof of his mouth—and he could smell, suddenly, beer, beer and this man's sweat, which he hadn't noticed before. "There now, don't cry," the man said when Pete stood up.

"I'm not crying." He backed up to the edge of the porch railing.

"That's a funny way to laugh."

"I'm not crying," Pete said. He wasn't.

He stared hard at the place where the flying saucer had disappeared. The ocean there was black and slick, and the white-caps were wiping out over and over again.

He could feel the man, Charlie Alexander, staring at his face. Pete didn't look at him. After a long time, he heard the crumpling of a beer can, and the man yawned loudly. He threw the smashed can on the pile. Altogether, there were six. Out of the corner of his eye, Pete saw the man stretch his arms over his head. "Boy, I'm bushed," he said. "You bushed? I'm bushed." He got up, put his hand over the grill. "I think this will be okay," he said. He winked at Pete. Then he put his finger on the grill, right on it. He held it there, grinning, then he held it up to Pete. He said, "Am I burning? You got to tell me if I'm burning or not because I got no feeling in my extremities." Pete could see a brown crease in his finger like a guitar player would have. This man had deliberately burned his finger. The man held his fingers to his nose. He said, "I'm burning. I think I am." Then he threw back his head and laughed.

Pete sat sideways on the porch, one foot on the top step, one on the next. He looked at the dark window in the downstairs apartment. The man hadn't turned any lights on. Not even the bathroom light, unless he was in there with the door closed. The lights worked. Pete's mom complained about how the electric bill was supposed to be divided between the two apartments, but there was no way to divide it when there was nobody downstairs to pay.

Pete picked up the leftover fish on the bag and threw it out beyond the grill. Cats would come and eat it, or coyotes. Pete had never heard of such a thing as an albino coyote. He'd like to see one, though. He wondered if he had the eye.

The apartment door was open, the screen closed. Pete couldn't hear Charlie moving around in there.

"This man," his mom would say, "is not in control of his circumstances. Keep an eye out."

Pete wanted good night vision. You had to practice to get it. When he and his dad used to go camping, his dad made him walk without a flashlight so he would learn how to listen. His dad had good night vision. Pete wondered if he'd ever seen an albino coyote. His dad would probably say that was hocus-pocus.

Once they were walking in a field and had come on something. His dad knew. Pete didn't. His dad put his hand on Pete's shoulder and they stopped, and then all around them the ground stood up. They had walked into the middle of a circle of wild horses. His dad said, "At night, you got to learn to listen with your ears and your eyes. When it's dark, people rely too much on their eyes and they don't hear everything." Later, though, when Pete was lying in his sleeping bag staring at the stars, he heard what his father had heard, the circle of horses breathing, and it was funny how he could remember hearing it but didn't hear it at the time. He was much younger then, though.

Last year he had seen a cat eating a skunk. He had woken in the middle of the night, had heard something—his father hadn't heard it. He got his flashlight and shone it on the sand, and there was a cat eating a skunk. He woke his parents up to show them. His mom said that the cat was sick and couldn't help itself. Something had made it crazy. She said that there were all kinds of circumstances that could cause people and animals to do unnatural things—like the people who had built a fire in the downstairs apartment. His mom said they were not in control of their circumstances, that they were probably hungry and cold and had been driven indoors by the weather, but his dad said that was nonsense. He said people didn't have license to destroy property because they were cold and hungry. He said people had to learn how to exercise a little control, but his mom said there were some things over which there was no control. They had fought about it. This was just before Pete's dad went north.

He'd said he was coming back with a bundle of money in case Pete's mom needed another operation, but his mom said his father would never come back, said it right to his face. "You won't come back because you can't stand to be around illness," she said.

His dad said that wasn't true. He told Pete he'd be back with a bundle, and that he'd call every Sunday, but yesterday was Sunday, and he didn't call.

Pete guessed that was hocus-pocus, too.

The fire down the beach had died to almost nothing, but the driftwood in the grill still glowed. He scooted down the steps to the bottom one, leaned out stretching his hand over the grill. He touched the very edge with his index finger but drew away before he could tell if it was hot or not. He touched it again—

"I wouldn't do that if I were you."

Pete jerked back and stood up. The man stood in the doorway behind the screen. He wasn't wearing a shirt.

"Shouldn't you be in bed?" he said.

Pete stuck his hands in his pockets and looked out toward the ocean.

"I think you probably should."

Pete kicked at the sand, kicked it hard so it spread onto the grill. He looked quickly at the man. The bottom half of the screen door was solid. He could see only his naked upper half. The man's eyes were tiny dark buttonholes in his face. Pete thought the bottom half was probably naked, too. His heart was thudding.

He took a step, then another. He had not heard him. How had this man sneaked up on him? Charlie Alexander. Pete's back prickled. "Hey, where you going?" the man said, his voice low, gruff—teasing.

Pete walked out beyond the grill, his neck and back prickling.

"Hey! Don't go!" Charlie Alexander laughed. "I don't bite."

Pete's shadow stretched before him on the sand, then sud-

denly disappeared. Too suddenly. The light behind him had
gone off. This man, this Charlie Alexander, had come out his
door, had opened the door at the bottom of the stairs, the door
that led to the upstairs apartment—their apartment—where
the light switch was, and turned the porch light out. Pete listened behind him. He tried to hear movement, feet on the
porch, but this man who was not in control of his circumstances could probably move as silently as a cat because crazy
people can sneak up on you, and Pete tried not to listen too
hard because if you listen too hard, your ears will play tricks
on you.

He walked toward the water, his flip-flops quacking against
his heels like ducks. He wanted to run, but crazy people can
always outrun you. As gently as he could, he kicked one shoe
off, didn't break stride, then the other, and left the ducks behind—he, grinning like a crazy person, too, couldn't help it.

At the place where the loose sand turned hard and sloped
down toward the water, he turned around and looked back toward the dark house. He could see nobody. He squatted. He
swiveled his head, looking along the line of trees behind his
house. He could see no human shape among the trees, no one
standing, no animal, either. He was pretty sure he could not be
seen. He was a head in the sand. He knew the exact point
where he disappeared, where he could squat in the sand and
see the house but not be seen. He had been a head in the sand
many times, watching his mom look for him. He could see
nothing on the shadowy porch, or in the house. Charlie
Alexander could be on the porch or in the stairway. He could
be in their apartment, but there was no light on up there.

When they had smelled smoke from the campfire in the
downstairs apartment, his mom had called the beach patrol,
who came and put the fire out and arrested the people. Afterward, his mom told Pete if he was ever trapped in the apartment and there was fire on the stairs, he should take his

chances and jump out the window because the sand was soft and he was a monkey. He would survive a fall but not a fire. His mom told him he had to be prepared for any eventuality.

A phone was ringing. It was a tiny little mouse ring from the tiny little upstairs in the tiny little house. It would be her, his mother. She would be mad that he didn't answer. She would call Lynn. That was a certain eventuality. Lynn would come in her truck and—he thought suddenly that Charlie Alexander could be on the stairs listening to his mom's voice, and blood rushed through him, made him hot.

He wanted to run back, to shoot the man—if he had a gun he would. Invisible baby fish flipped in his hands. He dug his fingers hard into his palms until he thought he could puncture himself, and then dug harder and gritted his teeth. He thought, I *have feeling in* my *extremities*.

His leg bones ached, so he dropped from his squat, kneeling in the wet sand, feeling the wetness seep into him. He knew a trick for staying awake. Cold water. Cold ocean water. Nobody falls asleep in cold water, his dad had told him. Once his dad threw cold water in Pete's face to get him out of bed. But Pete wasn't lazy anymore. He could stay awake all night.

This was a good distance. From here he could see just about everything, and nobody could sneak up on him because he had the cold ocean at his back. He would just watch until he saw Lynn's truck lights. Lynn would come. He knew his mother had called her, as sure as he knew his own name. When he saw headlights turn down their road from the highway, he would run hard and head his aunt off before she reached the house. He would run low, like a soldier. He would stay below the loose sand where Charlie Alexander couldn't see. If he was watching, he wouldn't know where Pete would come up. Even Pete didn't know. He knelt there, watching and listening, thinking about what he would do when he knew what must be done.

headhunter

The truck was climbing steadily onto ledges of sand, each one looking like the last. Ginny had seen few cars on this road and no animals, though she kept passing signs that cautioned her to watch for them. The inside of the cab felt like sand, and so did the inside of her mouth. The tops of her arms had separated into hundreds of little lines, and her hand, when she touched it to her tongue, tasted like salt. She had developed a twitch below her left eye, and her eyes were dry. The absence of moisture gave the landscape an edge, like glass.

She rolled down the window and let the air blow her hair. A white sign told her she was entering the largest antelope reserve in the United States. On the yellow caution signs the antelope had its front legs folded under it, very graceful in silhouette. There were blond rocks in the distance that could be animals wisely resting in the heat of the day. In places, the road had buckled and warped from the heat so the truck dipped and rose as it moved along.

Without looking, she reached for the water bottle beside her and twisted off the lid. The water was warm. She shifted legs, using her left for the gas, resting her right on the passenger's side. The little shrunken head hanging from her key chain knocked against her thigh. When she was eight, her father threw a nickel into a carnival dish and won the head for her. He said, "Now you'll always have something uglier than you."

She looked him in the eye and said, "This is my own sweet-faced friend."

While he threw the nickels she watched the Ferris wheel spin. She narrowed her eyes and made it spin off its axle. She made the people dangle out. She told her father that she wasn't afraid to ride, even though it might spin off, and he laughed.

"Bolted down pretty good," he said.

"God could make it," she told him.

"Well, yes," her father said, "but probably not tonight."

"Do not presume upon the Lord," she trilled in her high, sassy voice, and her father laughed; he spun her around and waltzed her through the crowd to the wheel.

Her father would be seventy years old on Saturday. The last time she had seen him, she watched him get up when her stepmother, Nan, left for a five-minute errand, pull his portable oxygen tank to the picture window, and stand there, rocking on his feet, until he saw Nan return. On the phone last week Nan had said, "He wants to be with me every minute of the day."

Ginny took another drink of water. Tonight she'd be in Medford. She'd sleep in her cousin's trailer. Tomorrow she'd drive north. On Saturday they would celebrate her father's birthday. She would be the surprise.

The plain suddenly dropped into a vast shadow on the left side of the road, and Ginny swerved hard to the right, then back, trying to correct. "Sweet Jesus!" she said. She tapped the brake with her left foot, twisted, and pulled her right foot back across the gearshift. She had been on a plateau. She hadn't realized. The cliff had come up so fast, and now she was driving down a mountain. She started to cross into the left lane. She wanted to see just how deep the canyon was, but a horn blasted, and she swerved back into her lane. He was around her before she could think. She hadn't known anybody was behind her.

She was shaking. She sat very straight, gripping the steering wheel, and her foot jerked on the brake. The land on her right was now a wall of shale that flaked and peeled; small blue-veined cracks cut into the wall, and fine desert sand ran from some of the cracks. At the base of the wall, sand hills nestled up against the shale, and they spread onto the highway, drifting across in a pink film.

The car ahead of her was green, an older model Ford Fairlane. The man driving had dark hair. He was a smallish man, only his head and the top of his shoulders visible from the rear. He was taking the curves more slowly now. Many of the curves were not marked, and those that were were marked with signs that had faded and cracked. The map legend showed this to be a regular state road, but clearly it was not maintained. In another ten years the pavement would be gravel or brush.

She downshifted to second. His brake lights glared, and she could smell her own brakes burning from the labored ride down the mountain. A thin line of blue smoke rose from his exhaust pipe. He began motioning for her to pass. He waved his arm slowly, as if directing traffic. She couldn't see, but he must be able to, so she pulled out, shifting to third. When she was even with him she looked at him. He was grinning at her.

She shifted to fourth, pulled in front of him, checked her rearview. He was waving, and now he put his hands together as if praying. She laughed. She knew his type. Her father used to tease her about such boys, even when she was too young to know what he meant. Each evening after supper she and her father used to walk to the train station, and they'd see the Mexican boys in their waxed-up cars, slicked-back hair, driving down Main, driving two fingered, the windows all open, and her father would say, "You want to watch out for joes like that," and she'd say, "Hubba, hubba."

"You going to go with joes like that?" he'd say.

"I might."

He'd look at her slyly out of the corner of his eye and give her hand a squeeze. "Well, just don't start anything you can't finish." He laughed then because he knew she didn't know a thing about it.

This old joe was tailgating her. Her speedometer crept toward forty-five, too fast for some of these curves. She braked, gently, then again. The man was close enough for their cars to kiss. She slowed further, put her hand out the window, motioned for him to pass. She saw gold shine in his mouth as he pulled out. When he was even with her he held something out across the seat. A bottle. The man was drinking. She shook her head. He nodded. She shook her head again, stepped on the brake, forced him ahead.

He pulled around, held the bottle up to his mirror, and she slowed to a crawl. He made a show of his bottle, waving it around, drinking from it, stepping on the brakes again and again and again, finally stopping and making her stop. He leaned his head out the window, held the bottle out and shouted something. She stuck her head out the window.

"Vinegar?" he said.

"Move it, you bugger."

The man opened his car door, started to get out, and Ginny hit him. Just a tap, but his car rolled forward, and the man leaped back in. He turned to look at her, incredulous. He shook his head, turned back around, hunched over the wheel.

Now he was going again. He began speeding down the mountain, and Ginny breathed deeply. She got the weird feeling, watching him stalk off, that he was having himself a tantrum. She watched his car sashay at the curves and then disappear around a bend.

She continued slowly, tapping her foot again and again on the brake. She saw him once, maybe a quarter-mile away, driving down the center of the road, taking his part of both lanes, and then she didn't see him at all.

She began to make out details in the field below, a tree, more a bush, there in the center of yellow weeds, weeds with tall, golden stalks. Angel fingers. That's what Nan called them. "Those aren't weeds, honey. Those are angel fingers." Her stepmother had a name for everything. Nan had a name for Ginny's little shrunken head. It was a grief bowl. "Do you know why the headhunter takes a head, Ginny? He is enraged. He needs a place to put his grief when he loses a loved one, so he takes an enemy's head." She had read that in one of her dream books. Nan had told Ginny she had not grieved properly for her mother when she died; Nan said Ginny would not be able to get on with her life until she faced her grief head-on. She told Ginny she must open the floodgates.

Nan was her mother's nurse just before she died, and afterward Nan would call on the phone to lend an ear to Ginny's father, though she always did all the talking. She always called at suppertime. Ginny would watch him listen while Nan talked and his food got cold. She would see his jaw tighten. She would see the two points of color come into his cheeks. He would answer Nan's questions with yeses and noes, and when he hung up he'd shake his head at Ginny and say, "Now there's another country heard from." They would laugh.

After the calls, though, he didn't want to eat anymore; he wanted to drink. But he never told her to stop calling, and a year after Ginny's mother died, he married Nan. By then he was drinking pretty good.

Once, late at night, after he remarried, Ginny's father came into her room, woke her up, and asked her if she wanted to talk about her mom. She knew Nan had told him to ask.

"No," she said. He nodded. He sat there smoking his cigarette until it was done, then kissed her head and left.

Ginny rounded a curve, and there was the man in the Fairlane directly in front of her, stopped dead in the road. She hit the brakes. He was leaning out the window, motioning with the bottle for her to pass. She would not. She would not let him get behind her again. She shook her head. He pulled back in, and his reverse lights came on. She jammed the gearshift into reverse, looked quickly behind her, began to back up. He backed up, too, closing the gap, hitting her, pushing her a few feet, and she thought she heard glass break, and she knew her front bumper had connected with his taillights. He stopped. They both stopped.

Ginny was shaking violently. Her arms and legs had turned to rubber, and she could feel sweat running down her sides, from her throat, and under her breasts. The guy sat there, his elbow crooked on the door, his head in his hand, his fingers drumming his head, as if he were waiting for a traffic light to change. The guy was crazy. She could hear nothing but her own engine. His, she thought, had stopped. She looked again and again into her rearview. A car coming up on her around the bend might not be able to stop. "Move it, you old joe," she said. They sat like that for a minute, two, and then she saw his door open again, and she saw his foot step out.

"Goddamn you!" she yelled, and she threw the gearshift into first, rammed him hard. His car leapt and the door snapped on him. He fell back in, and she rammed him, saw him sit up in the seat, begin yanking the gearshift, rammed him again, then jammed her foot on the brake, put her hand over her mouth, and watched the Fairlane slip over the edge of the mountain.

At the bottom of the hill she sat quietly in the truck, her hands hanging loosely on the steering wheel. Halfway across the field the underside of his car faced the road, and the wheels spun. The car was half buried by angel fingers.

She opened the truck door and stepped out. The stench of hot tar rolled up to her, and the pavement burned through the soles of her sandals. She crossed the road and stood at the edge of the field. She could hear the engine running and something knocking. Did she smell gas? She could not see a wet slick running over the car's innards, which were now exposed, nor could she see the details of the car's underbelly. She could see the two tires spinning. When the engine began to chug noisily and then abruptly died, the tires did not immediately stop.

She looked back up the mountain and then in the other direction along the flat stretch to where the pavement disappeared in a shining pool of light—the only sound the chattering of cicadas. She stepped from the pavement into the weeds. Grasshoppers shot out from under her, flying grasshoppers with armored backs, flashes of yellow and orange under the wings, hundreds of them that spread in waves, whispering past her bare arms and her ears, and she slapped at the air around her, then at her back when she felt the soft flutter of insect legs. She began to run, to bore through the weeds, which snagged at her hips and waist, crackled under her feet, but then she stopped. Yes. It was gas she smelled. Now she could see the blackened axle.

A spot of red on the mountain caught her eye, and she looked up. A car, a red sports car, had just begun its descent. It swung out at one of the top curves, then disappeared into a switchback, reemerged. She watched it weaving along gracefully, bending with the road. It moved so fast, darting in and out, the engine whining, then revving. It sounded like an angry hornet disturbed from its hive, chasing down the mountain, busy and mean—she ducked. She laughed nervously. She crouched flat-footed and held her knees. She did not look at the place where the car would emerge. She pressed her fists to her heart, and she strained toward the road, listening for the engine. She clenched her arms to her sides and clamped her teeth, though her own air hissed through them because she was laughing and could not help it. It was a good hiding place. She stared at her toes, the cracks and toenails defined by thin lines of red dirt. The weeds around her had brown spots, moving, twirling brown spots. Bile lurched in her throat. They were not worms. Cockroaches, she thought. They looked like the shiny backs of red and brown cockroaches hanging from the weeds and twirling toward her, though when they twirled at a certain angle she saw there were no legs or bodies. They were empty shells, flaking red pods, and some had fallen— some she had crushed under her feet, and one was alive. Near her right eye a cicada ate at the pod. She hit it. She stood and began winding her arms like windmills and slapping at herself, stopping suddenly and listening to her own breath rasp in her throat. The red car was not in sight. She held her elbows in her hands and scanned the road as far as she could see. Nothing moved.

She began walking. The weeds stank of gasoline. When she was little she had loved this smell. She would walk with her mother to the Conoco station to buy penny candy and to see her mother's friend, Sam. "Hey, Ginny," Sam would say. "How's tricks?" And she would say, "Just fine, just fine," and she would pull her hot pennies out of her pocket.

"Girls don't have to pay," Sam told her.

"Yes, they do," her mother said, and Sam would give her mother a look.

"Tell your mama to leave your daddy and run away with me," Sam told Ginny. All the time he said this.

"She won't," Ginny said.

"Your mama drives me crazy," Sam told her, and her mother would grin and lick her teeth. They would, she and her mother and Sam, sit by the pumps, eating red licorice and smelling the gasoline.

She began to circle the car. The whole back end was crumpled, the metal folding into a sort of grimace, and the window, though intact, was segmented into thousands of green squares, each square frosted in white. The top had dimpled but had not collapsed. The front window was gone. She could not see the man. She stepped closer. She could smell the gasoline and the acrid scent of alcohol and cigarettes. The upholstery, a dark green weave, was horribly shredded and curled into the foam. She thought he must be dead, or so deeply unconscious that his breathing was shallow.

She put her hand and then her head through the space where the glass would have been. "Yes?" she whispered. "Yes?" She was crying in her throat, but her eyes did not tear. She stared into the darkness below. Careful not to touch the jagged glass in the window frame, she lifted her leg and stepped on the ground where the driver's window should have been, leaning her calf against the steering wheel. She arched her back to avoid the glass shards, pulled her other leg in, scratching her knee against a piece of glass, and stooped so that no part of her head touched the passenger's window. She turned, stood flat-footed, looked over the seat into the back, and she tried to stop the sound in her throat.

At first she thought the coat piled against the back door was him. At first she took the crumpled armrest for his ruined face. She stared at these things, barely breathing, then scanned the whole back floor. He was not there.

She crossed her arms over her middle. It was, after all, just a little bit of a fall. She began to shake. She stared at the shattered glass in the back window. In the corner, tiny black beads swarmed a half-buried silver crucifix.

She turned her head slowly, painfully, toward the opening. She could see only the narrow alley of weeds and blue sky framed by the windowsill, and she strained to hear past the soft whisper of grasshoppers. The back of her head felt as though it was being pierced with iced pins. Ridiculous little popping sounds came from the engine, and she tried to hear beyond them. She leaned against the seat back, her cheek resting against exposed foam. She began to laugh silently, and tears squeezed out the sides of her eyes—

She slapped her right thigh, then her left, then dug both hands into her pockets. The keys were not there. She could see them, in her mind, dangling from the ignition. She began pushing her way out of the car, and glass tore the skin on her back and leg. Outside, she glared at the highway. Her truck was still there. She began to run. She must get there before he did because if he took her truck, he took everything. Now she was flying face-first into the weeds and she pushed herself up, ran again, stopped. She looked back. Her ears were throbbing. She turned and walked back.

He lay face-up, eyes closed. He was grinning that same wide-toothed, hubba-hubba grin he'd flashed when he offered the bottle. *Vinegar?* Her stomach lurched. His hips and legs were twisted horribly, his back flat on the ground. She could see no blood. She squatted. She stared at his chest, then at his mouth. She began to rock, gently, forward then backwards, stopped, reached over, and held her fingers above his mouth, then jerked her head around. She shuddered. He was not heading toward her truck anymore. He was not looking for her.

She felt the air over his mouth again, then dropped her hand until her fingers brushed the dry surface of his teeth and she could not see the grin, pressed, then jerked her hand away when she felt the teeth give, stood, and began to run across the field away from the mountain and the man.

She ran to the low hill opposite the mountain. She ran up the slope, her feet sliding in the sand. Not halfway up, she stopped and let the ground pull her back. She sat down and leaned back, settling into the earth, which burned her neck and shoulder blades, and she pushed into it until the burn faded and the ground below became indistinguishable from her own skin. She stared at the sky just over the mountain. She closed her eyes and saw him again, his face grinning back at her, the car rolling, never hesitating, disappearing.

A breeze had come up, blowing from the north, and she listened to the rustling of dried grass. Fine grit hung from her lashes, sand that looked like tiny dots of glass. She turned her head, testing the heat with her cheek. At her feet, a stick. She watched it sideways. A black speck crawled over the sand toward it. She closed her eyes, making the speck disappear, opened them, and there it was. She sat up. A lone black ant had begun its journey around the end of the stick. She picked the stick up and put it in the ant's way. The ant stopped. It backtracked. It began to detour. She blocked its way again, and it stopped again.

An anthill just to her left swarmed with the little ant's kin. She tossed the stick onto the hill but it rolled off. She scooted over, picked the thing up, and stuck it directly in the hole. Ants stormed up, climbing the stem as a unit, climbing onto each other as if there were somewhere to go. She pulled the stick out. She stared at the conglomeration on the end of the stick. "Now here's another country heard from," she said.

She thought of Sam, the Conoco man, her mother's old friend. "That one's a country unto himself," her father used to say about Sam. Once, Sam got moony-drunk and came to the door, stood with his arms open and said, "Anything you want," to her mother. Right there in front of her father. Her mother thought it was funny, but her father picked Sam up and threw him into the street. Her father had taken her mother's face in his hand then. He held her face for a long time, his eyes spooked and furious, and she stared back at him. Then he let go. A few days later, Ginny could see little blue prints on her mother's white cheek. They never mentioned it, but Ginny and her mother stopped going to the Conoco.

They had not known her mother was sick until a month before she died, and during that month, the phone rang every morning. Ginny would pick up the receiver and listen to dead space on the other end of the line. It was Sam. He wasn't saying anything, but he was there.

Nan said Ginny's mother wouldn't have died if she'd just opened her mouth and told somebody about the pain. That month her mother's hair turned thin as web, and the tip of her tongue began to split. She could not stand the touch of food or drink or medicine on her tongue. She used to ask Ginny to hold the mirror for her. "I'm watching myself disappear," she said, and when Ginny cried, she said, "It's nothing to cry about."

Ginny stood. She shook her legs, first one, then the other, dislodging the ants that had begun to crawl on her. She wondered when this all started. Now the sun was going down. The field shone, and ants sprinkled off the stick, catching and clinging to the golden stalks.

Though there was no noticeable indenture where his body was, she knew and walked straight to it. He had lost his shoes. His socks were dirty white. She thought of what Nan always said to her, first thing, before she even said hello: "Did you have any adventures on the drive? Did you meet anybody?" This time, she could say yes. Ginny laughed, and then she started to shake.

She walked to the man's head, kicked at the flies circling his face, dropped to her knees, and beat the air over his face, her fingers fluttering, then held her hands over his face until the flies began to light on them. She yelled at them and beat the air.

Had she done this?

The man's cheek under the cheekbone held a shadow. It curved beautifully so that a touch of blue defined cheekbone and jaw. She put her fingers there. His cheek was warm, though she felt the chill just under it. His skin was warm from the sun, not himself.

She wanted to go. She just wanted to be back on the road.

She stood. Two cars were passing each other near her pickup. She knew many had gone by. But she was invisible in the weeds, she and this man at her feet.

This would be a good hiding place. She could just go. She thought of her own country where she had grown up, on the western side of the Cascades. In the forest behind her house, each bush held an animal, and she knew they were there before she saw them; she went there so often that she could feel them before she saw them, even the gray squirrel hidden in the ash tree, and the green lizard camouflaged in ivy. Once she had come on the carcass of a deer. She did not smell it. It had long since ceased to smell. But she felt the chill in her bones just before she saw it. It was half hidden under a bush, and she would have missed it if she had not sensed where to look.

She looked at the body once more, stooped to wave the flies from the mouth. She could actually see where the teeth had loosened. The impact must've shaken them loose. One was missing completely, the roots half exposed in the others. The only one intact was the artificial one. The gold tooth shone in his gum like a fine jewel. She touched it with her index finger. It was dry. It did not seem to be loose. She laughed, folded her arms around her, looked at the empty field. Nobody was looking for her. She poked the tooth again. Why wasn't anybody looking for her? She took hold of it. She was shivering, suddenly, every part of her, shivering. She held the tooth near the gum, wedged her fingernails into the gum line, yanked, felt it give. "Jesus!" she said, standing and stepping back. The tooth dipped into the mouth. The tongue, she saw, was black, and the gold hung above it, dangling over the dark cavern, then turned black itself when a fly lit on it—

"Goddamn," she said, kicking the fly away. She dropped to one knee, putting her right foot on the ground for leverage, pulling, digging under the tooth on the inside, pushing her fingers up into the roof of his mouth, pressing there until she no longer felt the smooth skin. All that she felt was the bone. From the pit of her stomach, a thin animal sound rose. She reached up into this man's mouth to the place where the gold began, pushed back on his skull with her other hand, pulled, and the sound rose to a wail. The cicadas trilled with her in one last song before the sun set.

In the low-lying hills that lead into the Cascades, the air smelled of wet hay, animal dung, and smoke. She drove half sleeping, her foot stationary on the pedal, two fingers on the wheel, watching the edge of the blacktop, which curled off into the hills. The hills steamed from the day's heat. Though she could distinguish little in the dank land, she could feel the grass and crops oozing around her, and now and then her headlights glanced off a black slick that would be a pond on the roadside. Her windshield had begun to catch bugs, their white goo spreading in arcs when she used the wiper, until halfway through the Cascades she noticed that the glass had turned the color of milk, and she stopped to clean it, digging at the masses that had dried. She listened behind her to the land twitching as it cooled. When she drove, she half dreamed about the time passing. Because she did not have a watch, she made her own time, estimating minutes and hours by mileage posts, keeping track of each little town and adding it in, though she was less interested in getting to Medford than in clocking the places where she had been. This was the sort of thing her father was interested in. He would ask her, "Which way'd you come?" and "How long did it take you?" She wondered what he would look like now. Nan said he had lost weight. "Come home and cheer your father up," Nan had said.

On the western side of the Cascades, her headlights caught the silver threads of moss hanging from the trees around her. They looked soft and soothing, like silk shawls hanging from the trees, or like her own mother's hair, which had turned silver in a day, so it seemed. When Ginny and her mother used to do the dishes, her father would come up behind them and lift the hot hair from their necks. "You're one slick chick," he always told her mother, and her mother would nudge Ginny. "You know what that makes you? One slick chicken." Her father would say, "I guess it's the other way around."

Every night he kissed the back of their chicken necks.

An hour outside Medford it began to drizzle. She cracked the window and put her fingers out, letting them soak in the air. Tonight, she'd sleep in her cousin's trailer, and the rain would beat against the metal. In the morning she'd drive north. She was going to cheer her father up. She would be the surprise. They would sit at the kitchen table together and drink the whiskey she was bringing. She'd say, "I didn't know what to get you," and then they'd get drunk.

And she'd say, "Pop, I have a secret."

He'd say, "What is it?"

She'd say, "I can't tell you because then it wouldn't be a secret anymore."

He'd say, "Dad blast it."

In this way, she would cheer him up. She could make him grin because she was his own sweet-faced girl.

dr. war is a voice on the phone

Dr. War is a voice on the phone, he says, "Come on, baby, let's fight."

I say, "I don't mind."

He says, "What's your address?" Then I go out on the curb to wait.

While I'm waiting I try to imagine what he looks like. I try to imagine from the six times I've talked to him on the phone. He says, "How old are you? Are you twelve?" he says. "What do you look like? Like, is your hair long or short," things like that, he asks me, and, "Do you like to dance?"

I asked him how he got my number. He says, "It's a mystery how. Things like that spring up from the earth."

The third time he called I almost walked through the sliding glass door to answer. I was out back, and Aunt Tiel's yelling, "Bring me some orange juice," or, "Bring me a Bloody Mary." Tiel got her hair shaved off below the belly. She showed me the naked crack, saying, "Smooth like a baby's," but it's stubbled like a man's face. She said, "What do you think of that?" I don't think much of it. Of Tiel, flat on her back with memory loss. She comes home from the hospital, she says, "They took from me what it means to be a woman and threw it in the trash can." She says, "I don't remember what it means to be a woman," and says, "Bring me a Bloody Mary."

I have dark hair, if you're interested. Some people think it's thick. I rub it in the grass out back. I wonder what Dr. War will think of that. He said, "Did you ever let a boy kiss you, and did you take your shirt off for him?" When my uncle said, "Let's cut the rug, Dina," and we held our two hands under my chin, I took my fingers and unbuttoned my top button while we were dancing. I did this. I danced with my button undone. He didn't notice.

I'm sitting here on the curb waiting for my ride. He says, "What are you wearing right now? Like, are you wearing a dress or shorts, and what color?" I don't tell him everything. The length of this skirt, I didn't say, just the color, red. The number on this house I didn't tell, just the street. Let him find me. Let him open his eyes and look. He could be any one of these passing by, slowing down and passing by.

I have come outside from my uncle's house while bald Tiel talks to the TV and my uncle snores in his chair. I have rubbed my head on the grass, and electrified hair flies from my face. I don't know who Dr. War is. He just called me on the phone. He could be any one of these.

the hypnotist's trailer

A woman, Josephine, read an ad in the local advertiser one day: ADDICTION THERAPIST. CAN CURE ANYTHING. HYPNOTISM; PSYCHIC MASSAGE. Josephine smoked; she'd tried to stop. She drank a little bit, too, maybe a little more than she should. She decided to give the hypnotist a try. She took her daughter along for moral support.

The hypnotist lived and worked in a trailer on a paved lot at the base of Stone Mountain. He was a hairy man but his teeth were straight and his fingernails clipped. His place was sparsely furnished—a rattan couch, a tweedy chair. No little vases, no magazines. "No distractions, no regrets," the man said, waving Josephine and her daughter to their seats. Then he said it again, looking deeply into Josephine's eyes. "No distractions, no regrets." His voice was soothing, and the couch was soft. In no time at all, Josephine slipped into a deep hypnotic trance.

"Let's skip the preliminaries and get right down to it," the hypnotist said. "Do you believe in God?"

"Yes," Josephine said.

"What does he look like?"

This confused her.

"Does he have a beard?"

"Oh, yes."

"I have a beard."

"Yes, you do."

"He has long hair and brown eyes, too."

Josephine supposed he did.

In short order, the hypnotist convinced her that she was in the presence of God.

"Do you believe that God can deliver you from your sins? Will you put your trust in the Lord?"

She did. She would.

"Give me a token of your trust, then."

"Token?"

"Something you value. Your purse, perhaps."

The daughter—Irene was her name—laughed, and a shadow crossed the hypnotist's face. He glanced at the girl. She was pretty in a trashy way. Her face was white with makeup, and her eyes were lined in green. She wore her hair in that half-shaved, half-dyed style he hated. She was a skinny thing, though. He liked skinny things, and he felt a sudden urge to involve her.

"Your daughter was right to laugh," he said. "A purse is just a thing."

Josephine smiled at the girl; Irene rolled her eyes.

"Give me something you truly value," the hypnotist said. He winked at the girl. "Give me your daughter."

Irene laughed. "Yeah, Mom. Give me to him."

"My daughter?" Josephine frowned. Since reaching puberty, Irene had become a difficult child. Josephine looked at the hypnotist, who was stroking his beard, eyeing the girl. To her surprise, the man's face began to change—to lose its rough and flabby cheeks and nose, to smooth and tighten into somebody she knew. She blinked and there he was, the juvenile detention officer who had, in recent years, begun to haunt her porch and frequent her dreams.

Suddenly she threw her arms around Irene. "You can't have her!" she hissed.

The hypnotist raised his eyebrows, then looked at his feet.

"It's all my fault she's bad," Josephine whispered.

"I can see that," he whispered back.

Irene slipped out of her mother's grasp. She liked being noticed but was growing a little bored. She began looking around, kicking her foot, generally fidgeting. The hypnotist frowned. Boredom was not good. Boredom broke the mood. He ran his tongue over his teeth, leaned forward, smiled at Josephine, and said, "Give me your bellybutton." Irene stopped kicking.

"What?" Josephine said.

"Give me your navel."

The girl grinned. This she liked.

"Give it to me," he whispered.

The woman looked down. She lifted her shirt, pushed down her skirt, and looked at it. What did he mean, give it to him? Was it like what you did with kids when you pretended to take their noses? She looked at her daughter. Irene nodded. Her daughter was naughty, but she was not evil. It must be like what you did with kids. Josephine laughed. She reached down and grabbed her bellybutton. To her surprise, it came off in her hand. She stared at it, horrified. It was flat as a penny, but as she watched the ends began to curl up. She gasped.

"Good," the hypnotist said.

She pushed it against her middle, trying to reattach it. Her ears were ringing. It wouldn't stay.

"Only God can put it back," the hypnotist said. "You see. You didn't trust after all."

"I didn't," she wailed. She held the navel in her right hand.

Her throat had thickened, and her temples were throbbing. She felt like crying.

"I will take good care of it because I believe you value it. Do you hear what I'm saying to you, Josephine? I believe you."

She looked at him. "You believe me?"

"I believe you, and I believe in you!" He said this with such conviction that her throat opened and tears came to her eyes. He believed her!

"Let me see it for a minute," he said.

"See it?"

"Just for a minute."

"Why?"

"To heal it. It's dying. Look at it."

She opened her hand. The navel had curled up into a little ball. It was brown and wrinkled like a rotten apple. Her hand began to shake.

"Here." He covered her hand with both of his. "There, there," he said. "Now I have it. It's okay." And he began to stroke it.

She watched closely. At first, she could see no difference, but then she noticed that the color was changing. Was the color changing? Yes! The color was fading, and the thing was growing. It was, with each stroke, flattening out to its original shape, and it was turning a sort of peach-ish. She smiled. He was fixing it.

"Now," he said, "how's that? Better?"

"Yes," she whispered. She held out her hand, but he did not give it back.

"I want to talk to you about something, Josephine. I want to talk to you about addiction."

"Oh," Josephine said. She sat back in her chair. She knew whatever he was going to say was right. She drank too much. She smoked too much. She laced her fingers over her stomach. Without her navel, she felt a little naked.

"Addicts don't have centers. They've given up their centers and replaced them with smoke. Did you notice how easily this came off?" She swallowed. "That wouldn't happen in a healthy person. Every piece of your body is in serious decay because of the way you have abused yourself, and when you abuse your-self, you abuse everyone around you. Your family—" He looked at the girl. She had her elbow on her knee, her chin in her hand; she was absorbed by something outside the window.

"But in a healthy person, the center is vibrant; it's elastic. Shall I show you?" He began to wave his hand over the navel. "Watch it," he whispered. The little thing in the middle of his palm began to throb and fill with color. He touched its edges. He licked his finger and ran it around the rim. He looked at Irene. She was really a very pretty girl. He admired the haughty turn of her head, the regal line of her ear, the curve of her jaw—the awkward neck, the long and turtleish neck that would, when she was older and fatter, lose its sinewy grace but now turned elegantly at the clavicle. He followed the line of her neck under the skimpy halter to the bare and pointed shoulder, down to the rose tattooed on her arm, back up to the shoulder and down along the teenage breast, which curved nicely, not too full, not too flat, there against the thin cotton. He closed his eyes and ran his finger slowly along the lip of the navel. "Look," he whispered. "Watch me make it grow."

Josephine, watching, saw her navel turn a translucent white, the color of a communion host, a shimmering world from a cold and beautiful night—God's night—and it had grown. When he held it at a certain angle, tilted slightly toward her, she saw the moon and herself reflected in it. It was hers! She laughed.

The hypnotist opened his eyes. He looked at the mother, at her slack jaw and gleaming eyes, and he laughed, too. "Look," he said. He twirled the thing on his finger. "Watch this." He tossed it in the air, and it began to wobble, to redden, and, when the hypnotist pushed a button under his chair, to smell a little like the perfume counter at Woolworth. The disk was changing from orange to red to pink, undulating, and Josephine began sliding up and down in her chair, and her skirt hiked up. He stared at her thigh. It was a nasty little thigh, plump and unmuscled, just the way he liked them. "Stand up," he commanded. "Turn around."

Irene glanced from the window to see her mother dancing in slow, snaky circles, running her tongue over her lips, rubbing her hands over herself, her mother! A reserved woman. Her mother was from a line of reserved women. Even when she was drunk, her mother would wander around the house tucking things in. But now she began catching her skirt and pulling it up, shimmying up and down, and the man's tongue was resting between his teeth. His eyes were little beads in his face. "Bend over," he whispered. Josephine bent at the waist and shook her head between her knees.

"Mom?" Irene said.

The hypnotist leaned back in his chair, clasped his hands behind his head, and said, "Well, hello, Josephine."

"Hey!" Irene said. The man glanced at the girl. Irene glared stonily at him, and he sneered. He looked her up and down, then looked into her eyes and saw his own reflection, an ugly fat man. He looked closer. Stared into the coal black contempt of a young girl's eyes and saw himself as she saw him—a flabby-skinned, dim-eyed, feeble-gummed half-man, looked further, then, and saw the man he would become: his lips began to turn inward and his skin to hang like rags from his sharpened cheekbones, his eye sockets to protrude, and his eyes to sink. Irene, caught in his stare, saw his shoulders begin to bow, his chest under his shirt to sink, his hands and lips and head to shake. His aged face was a mesh of tiny broken blood vessels, blue and red, and his eyes were pupilless pools of pain, dank, sludgy bogs oozing tears—yes, the creases below his eyes were wet, and she heard him whisper, though his lips did not move: "When you reach a certain age," he said, "there's nothing left but tears."

Irene's young throat constricted, and her heart was moved to pity; she heard a bird call and began to notice a faint odor in the room—a little like the perfume counter at Woolworth.

The hypnotist glanced out the window at the mountain with its colorless surface and stone-cold center, at this scenic stupor where they'd made him park his trailer, and suddenly an old hatred welled within him. He had once been famous, but he had offended by revealing little truths, dirty little secrets, and they had exiled him. They had taken from him his best years. *His* had not been a sleight-of-hand talent. *He* was no trickster, no two-bit juggler, no smoke-and-mirrors hack. He had studied, he had watched, he had learned the ways of the human heart and mind, had found the secret chambers of fear and delight, and when he performed he stood before his audiences a naked man, but he was *with* them. He did not perform: He lived! He had been untouchable, and they hated him for it, and so they left him here.

He looked at Josephine, whose face was beet red, whose eyes were mostly pupil. He curled his lip.

"Okay, now," he whispered, and the woman straightened. She smoothed her skirt, perched on the couch, put her fingers to her lips, glanced cautiously at her daughter, who seemed to be listening to something. Josephine shivered.

"Okay. Now, watch it shrink." Josephine sat back and watched. The hypnotist took down the moon, which had been hovering over his head, and began to fold it in triangles, each triangle smaller than the last, and when it was the size of his hand, he began to mold it into a glowing sphere. He covered it with his other hand, closed his eyes, opened them, opened his hand, and there was her navel again, a perfect little peach disk, flat as a penny but with the little spiral in the middle. He smiled and held it out to her. She started to reach for it when he opened his fingers. "Oops," he said. "I dropped it." He laughed an ugly laugh.

"You dropped it?" Josephine said.

"Where'd it go?" he said.

"You dropped it?" she said again, and there was a tremor, something that could have been fear, or perhaps anger, in her voice.

"Where is it?" he said.

Josephine was staring at the floor. "*I* don't know," she said. She dropped to all fours. She began heaving, then hiccupping and sobbing. "Renie, it's lost."

"What's lost?" Irene shook herself, rubbed her eyes, saw her mother crawling around on the floor.

The hypnotist lifted his foot. Josephine looked at his shoe, then at the floor under his shoe, then, in horror, at the shoe as it crashed down on the floor. She jerked up. Her hands flew to her stomach. She gasped and the hypnotist laughed. "The automatic reflex of an amputee," he said. "Mama's going to dream tonight," he said. Josephine's lips were trembling. Her eye had begun to twitch, her shoulders to heave.

"Well, honey," the man said, "why'd you give it to me if you were only going to take it back?" He grinned. "All sales are final!"

He picked his foot up, studied the bottom of his shoe, seemed to scrape something off the bottom, winked at Josephine. He popped the thing in his mouth. Josephine's mouth dropped open and her eyes bulged.

"What's lost!" Irene demanded.

The hypnotist shrugged. "Everything," he said. His right cheek poufed like a chipmunk's. "I have eaten the plum she gave me. It was cold," he said. "So delicious." He opened his mouth, fluttered his purple tongue. And then he swallowed. He sat back and licked his lips. "Another satisfied customer."

Irene scowled. "Nothing's lost, Mom."

Josephine was clutching her stomach as if she had been run through with a sword, and the hypnotist was grinning. When had he felt so good? He leaned forward, shielded his mouth with his hand, and whispered a little secret to Josephine. "She's right, you know. It's not lost. Looky here. It's in the cuff of my pant."

Josephine sagged against the couch. She stared miserably at the little disk he fished from the cuff.

"Let's go, Mom," Irene said.

"Go?" Josephine said. "We can't go."

"She can't go," the hypnotist agreed. "I got her gumption."

But Irene was tired of this. Why had she come? She didn't want to come. Josephine had begged her to come. *Be my courage*, Josephine had said. She was always having to be Mama's courage. *That's what daughters are for*, Josephine liked to say.

Irene stood. "I'm going," she said.

"Going?" Josephine said.

Irene, hands fisted, stood over her mother. She teetered in that is-it-almost-over-I-can't-stand-any-more-of-this posture that she knew her mother hated. Josephine, looking up, saw Irene poised for flight. Poised in that if-you-don't-pay-attention-to-me-right-now-you'll-regret-it stance. Josephine frowned.

Suddenly, Josephine wanted a drink. She couldn't deal with the girl anymore.

She wanted a smoke. She began digging around in her purse but then remembered why she was here. Wasn't he supposed to do something about this? She frowned at the man. He leered at her. Her stomach flipped.

It was getting late, though, and she wanted a smoke. She stood up. Her legs wobbled. Her head spun. She clutched her purse with both hands and walked carefully to the door. She felt as if her parts didn't quite connect.

"Go?" the hypnotist boomed.

Josephine looked back at him. The man's eyes smoldered, and she shuddered.

"Aren't you forgetting something?" he said.

Josephine moistened her lips. But Irene had her hand on the knob, and when the door opened, Josephine saw the man's eyes grow wide. *How sweet*, she thought. *He doesn't want me to leave.*

The air in the room was rotten with perfume. The hypnotist stared at the door. White-knuckled, he gripped his chair. His lips twitched spastically into something that wanted to be, and then was, a smile. "Go?" He threw his head back and laughed. "Need not be present to win!" he shouted.

He looked from the door to the little hairs on his knuckles, turned his left hand over. With eyes half closed, he gazed at the center of his palm. The skin was yellowish, thick, though as he watched it began to change, to bubble, tumorlike. Gradually, the skin tightened and stretched and seemed to crack. A glowing disk, flat as a penny, worried its way to the surface.

The hypnotist held it up to his eye. There was a pinpoint hole at the center, and he stared through it at the door and laughed again. He tossed the disk into the air, caught it. "Heads or tails?" He slapped it hard onto the back of his hand. "Tails. You lose." He ground the thing into his hand, then watched it emerge on the other side.

Was that the whisper of wheels on pavement? "Back again?" He cocked his head and smiled at the door. But he heard no humming engine. The little disk quivered.

The six o'clock sun filtered through the blinds, scissoring the couch where the woman had sat. The trailer was quiet. He listened for the birds, but the birds never sang in the six o'clock heat. He frowned at the door. "Well, aren't you the little flirt," he said.

He got up, walked to the door, opened it, looked out into the cellophane waves that shimmied above the asphalt. Hot, stinky tar bubbled up through cracks at the base of his stoop. There was no one on the lot but him. There was no one in the drive.

"Gone?" he said. He shrugged. "Oh, well."

Really, he blamed himself. He was always going too far. A little rambunctious, that's what he was. Always had been. He chuckled at himself, at the way he was. And he was so sure he'd get lucky today—if not with the girl, then the mom. "Just shows you never can tell," he said.

In the palm of his hand, he held the disk over the asphalt. "If you don't want it," he shouted in the direction of the road, "I don't, either." With the index finger of his left hand, he flicked the disk.

It jiggled.

He flicked it again.

It jiggled.

He pushed it hard with the ball of his thumb, then shook his hand vigorously.

The little peach, grown sticky in the heat, clung to him.

He stepped back into the room, closed the door. His hands were gooey with it. "Down the drain you go," he said, heading toward the bathroom, but stopped. It seemed, somehow, larger. Had it grown? Could it have? Irritated, the thing sat, swollen and flaming, in the ball of his hand, and it smelled! Did it stink? He put it to his nose and sniffed. An odor, surely blood, the suffocating stink of blood-laced perfume, spoiled the air, and his hand itched. He scratched. The thing throbbed. It was a throbbing itch, and his fingers, he saw with horror, were swelling. He tried to make a fist but the fingers, each of them, were red and pregnant and didn't want to close. And perhaps . . . His eyes weren't so good anymore.

Yes, tiny blue veins laced the crusted edges of the thing in his hand. He began to tremble. When he looked closely he saw that the veins extended beyond the thing and into . . . Into?

Like a small boy, he put his hand behind his back. The birds were singing again. The thing was pulsing. *Into him?* His ears were ringing.

"Now you see it," he murmured. "Now you don't." He gasped.

It was gone. He felt it leave! He pulled his hand from behind his back. His palm was flat and yellow. He laughed, and then he hiccupped because there it was again, a slimy, pulsing, growing gob.

"Nowyouseeit, nowyoudon't!"

It jiggled, little belly laugh. The birds twittered.

This was wrong. He held it upside down, shook his hand, shook it vigorously, but the more he shook, the bigger it got. He stopped shaking. Sweat beads rolled along his fat lines. *She—*

Shouldn't have given it. What was she thinking? To give such a thing!

Then why'd you take it, dummy, he couldn't help but think, *if you were only going to give it back? All sales final!*

He slumped into his chair. He felt like crying, and he felt like laughing. Well, this was something new, at least. He stared at the wad in the palm of his hand. "Are you my little wife?" he said. He ran his finger over the thing, which was now, clearly, a translucent, pulsing membrane. He shuddered. "Are you my love?"

bitterwater

I'm not the sort of person who takes satisfaction in being scared to death. Some like it. They'll go to horror films for pleasure. I can't understand that. I've walked out of nearly every horror film I've gone to. My dad says life is scary enough; he tells war stories about being an Air Force navigator in World War II, how nothing you can imagine actually feels like being up in the air—no boundaries but air, and the bullets coming at you are real. But after I lived a bit with Manny, I thought he *could* imagine it, and better. Maybe he had something wrong with him. He was always on edge, like his whole person was this fighter plane with air boundaries and the bullets coming at him were real.

When I married Manny, it broke my dad's heart. Manny got in my head the day I met him. I was thirteen. My family had just moved to the Navajo reservation. A bunch of us played softball next to the Kerr Magee housing compound. Manny wasn't a company kid, but he came over anyway with his friends. Manny pitched. When I came up to bat, he stood on the mound and started tossing the ball in the air. He was chewing his gum, tossing the ball, chewing his gum, and then he started singing: "Walking down a country road in Tennessee, I met a little girl . . ." He got me laughing. He put his hands and the ball behind his back, closed his eyes like he was in choir, and sang that entire country song. I was rolling on the ground when he finally threw the ball. "That's strike two hundred and three," he said. He kept count of all the strikes he never got on me.

"You cheat," I told him.

Manny walked right up to me in the batter's square. He said, "I'm hurt. You have hurt me very bad." He told me that when I hurt him, I hurt his ancestors. Manny was Todacheene clan, which means Bitterwater. He was named for his clansman, Manuelito, the last great Navajo chief, who watched over him, just like God, so now a great chief's feelings were probably hurt. "The only thing to do," he said, "is get some money from your dad so we can go get a hamburger."

My dad wouldn't give me more than enough for one hamburger, though. He said, "That boy's got money. The government gives them money."

Manny said, "That's all right, Brenda. Buy one, and you can watch me eat."

Watching Manny eat was a thing. This was a wide, pancake-size hamburger from the Dog House, a skinny sliver of gray meat with two tiny dots of pickle and a squirt of mustard packed between two fat buns. I mean, a Dog House hamburger is mostly bread. But watching Manny eat—he's got these fingers that lace together over the top of bread like they're comfortable there. He's got his elbows propped on the table and a loose hug on this hamburger, and he looks happy, a boy with an appetite and the time to enjoy it, the way he watched me over that bread—and talked nonstop—and sort of just chewed at the same time, and smiled, and never offered me a bite. The way his jaw worked—man-faced muscles popping near his ears, some secret jaw action communicating something to the brain, and from the look in his eyes it could've been something dirty, like that meal was an illegal thing. I mean, he knew how to get a girl's attention.

I watched him all that year, and he watched me back. Then one night—this was when I was fourteen—he called me on the phone. "Hey, Brenda, you know who this is?"

"Yeah, I know who this is."

"This is Manuelito, in case you don't know."

"I do know."

He wanted to know what I was doing.

What I was doing was watching my dad be a stone in his chair. Mama had been telling him that there was nothing for her to do in the sticks. She wanted to take a correspondence course and become an interior decorator. My dad had been telling her how easy it was for people to hoodwink her, how she was a pushover for scams, and she was saying, "Daniel, this is a fully accredited correspondence course," and he was saying, "We been down that road before." Daddy thought if Mama really wanted something to do, she could come out and do the books at the mill. When he said that, she said, "Oh, happy day," and he stopped talking. Now he was just sitting there, and my mom was asking if she was part of his scenery. "Am I a tree?" she said, and raised her arms and fluttered her fingers.

I told Manny I was watching my mom be a tree.

Manny said, "Sneak out, and let's go for a drive."

So I went to bed early and sneaked out the window, and we went driving around, looking for action, but there wasn't any, so we sneaked back in through the garage. My dad had converted one quarter of the garage to a playroom. Everybody was asleep at the other end of the house and couldn't hear us out there. I got whiskey from dad's stockpile. Daddy laid in a stash once a month since you couldn't buy it legal on the reservation. Manny and me drank the whiskey with Coca-Cola, listened to KWIK, and sort of played on the couch.

At first, I was nervous. Manny wasn't. "Nobody knows I'm here," he said. "We won't get caught." He sang along with the radio—"Don't let me cross over . . . love's cheating line"—just singing in my ear, and I'm laughing, you know, and Manny's trying to find his way through my clothes, and what are you going to do? He had this way of getting around me.

Playing on the couch was what we liked best that winter, but then, my dad walked in on us once—I guess maybe I didn't have a shirt on—and Daddy was pale, and kicked Manny out, and told me I was grounded for the rest of my life. Manny wasn't afraid of my dad. He joked, and my dad heard this— "Hey, Brenda, if you ever get off the ground again, come on over."

I was seventeen when I married Manny. My dad didn't come to the wedding. We got married in the little hundred-year-old Catholic church the Franciscans built. Mama cried all through it, loud and soggy, and every time Father Bernard turned his back, Manny whispered words from Johnny Cash's song "Mama Cried" and I was cracking up.

Daddy didn't come to the wedding, but he came to the church. When we went out, he was sitting on the steps. He didn't speak to me; he spoke to Manny. He said, "You're going to need a job." He told Manny if he wanted a job, he had one at the mill. Manny thought that was real nice. He invited Daddy to come over to the chapter house for mutton and frybread.

Daddy eyeballed him, then me, then started walking toward the car.

"You don't like mutton?" Manny said.

Daddy looked back. "We'll start you out on the graveyard shift," he said. "Eleven to seven."

Manny said, "I don't mind the grave."

Daddy shook his head. I know what he was thinking. He was thinking Manny had an attitude problem.

I said, "He's just kidding."

Daddy said, "I better not find him drinking up there."

We lived in a house on Manny's aunt's property, back behind the company houses, right up against the bluffs. There was an old graveyard up there. Once, when we'd only been married a few months, Manny and me were walking up there. It was cold that day, November, and the sand was blowing, that fine grit that gets between your teeth. It was fenced off, but you could lift the barbed wire and climb in. Navajo graveyards are raggedy places, full of tumbleweeds. There were no headstones, but wooden crosses here and there, and in two or three places, plastic flowers. I didn't think anybody got buried there anymore. You couldn't tell who had been buried there because there were no names on the crosses. When we were kids we joked about robbing those graves—we company kids always played cops and robbers on the bluffs—and we believed that if anyone actually did rob an Indian grave he would get something, because we'd heard the Navajos buried people with all their wealth, jewelry, and blankets. But once I stepped on a grave, and the ground was rotten and my foot fell through. I touched a casket. It scared me. "I thought I touched bone," I told Manny the day we went up there. I hadn't been there since I was thirteen.

"You could have broken a leg," he said.

"I know it."

"You ever seen those old Navajo women that limp around?" he said. "My grandmother limps. Some say they used to break a girl's hip when she was a baby so she couldn't work. It's because the Utes would steal a Navajo girl and sell her for profit, but not if she couldn't work."

"That's cruel," I said.

"It was cruel," he said. "I don't know who came up with that idea. I hate it that they broke my grandmother's hip. But I would break yours," he said.

"Why don't you run across that graveyard for me?"

"You're crazy," I said.

Manny put his boot on one strand of the barbed-wire fence. He pulled another up with his hands making a gap big enough for a person to enter.

"You want to," he said. Manny wasn't teasing. He was like that. One minute he was joking around, the next, this stranger. His face was pasty, almost white, like he had painted it.

"I don't want to," I said.

He said, "Run across the fucking graveyard, or I'll break your fucking hip."

You know, there's no place else to go, really, up there. It's just a row of bluffs, sand pile after sand pile, maybe a child on a horse and the child's sheepdogs that will tear you limb from limb. Up on the bluffs there's no place, really, to go.

"It's just a game," he said, and he didn't care that I didn't want to, but pushed me through the barbed wire, and my arm ripped from one barb. Once when we were making love, Manny had stopped and said, "You know, I could take your clothes and put you outside and then everybody would see you. You want everybody to see you?" I felt so cold when he said that. I didn't want him to touch me anymore, and I pushed him away and said I didn't want to finish it. Manny thought this was hilarious. He lay on his back and laughed at the ceiling until I tried to choke him, and he thought that was even funnier, and I laughed right back until I was dead with screaming at him.

That day on the bluffs I felt as though he'd put me naked on the other side of the door. I was afraid of him that day, so all I wanted to do was turn around, walk through the barbed wire, through him, through the whole damn reservation, but he twisted me around and whispered, "Run or I'll break your fucking hip."

I walked. Manny had yelled, "Do I have to come in there?" and then I couldn't move. Manny yelled, "Jump." I'm standing in the middle of this graveyard. My husband is telling me to jump up and down. He says he wants to see if I'll fall through.

I sat down, right there in the middle of that graveyard. I knew that he wouldn't come in after me. I knew that Manny was too afraid of something in there to come after me. I thought I was safe sitting on those Indian graves.

He hated to be alone, so the graveyard shifts were a bad idea. I guess he was spoiled in that way. He needed a lot of attention. There was nobody to perform for up there at the mill in the middle of the night, just the ore roasters, usually, and Manny. He got a little crazy when he had to be alone. Like, he came home from work one morning, put both hands on my face, and said, "Brenda, do you think you're flesh and blood?" I could smell he had been drinking.

I said, "My dad'll fire you if he catches you drinking on the job."

"What do you think is flesh and blood if not you, Brenda?"

I told him I thought he should get a day job. That he wasn't around people enough the way he had to sleep during the days, and he didn't talk to anybody at night.

"Oh, I talk," he said. "You know what uranium is?"

I knew what uranium was.

"There's a thousand little bombs going off in those furnaces every night, and we have us some discussions. We talk about you, sweetheart. You're the main thing on my mind, you know that?" He hadn't just been drinking, he was drunk. "Of course, they don't listen. Here's how it is." He pulled out a kitchen chair and straddled it. "This is me," he said. He pointed at himself. "This is furnace one." He pointed at his right leg. "Imagine it's a metal box with uranium inside, and the fire's going nineteen hundred degrees," he said. He started stomping his right foot. "This is furnace two." He pointed at his left leg. "Imagine it's a metal box." He started stomping with that foot. He had both feet hammering against the kitchen floor, making a racket. Then he started speaking in Navajo, looking at the ceiling. There was a lot of noise in that kitchen.

"I listen to you," I yelled at him. "Who else am I going to listen to? You want all the goddamn attention."

He said, "Let's go to bed."

I told him I didn't want to.

He told me a man needed sex. But I didn't want to.

He got like that. But, too, he was a charmer. You have to love a man like that and mostly not mind his moods. When we were still kids, just married, Manny came home from work one morning with a pink bird under his arm, one of those plastic things you see in people's yards, and I had seen this particular plastic bird in the high school principal's yard forever. Manny had stolen it on his way home from work. He put it in the middle of the kitchen table, and the bird had breakfast with us. Manny said, "Baby, I brought you the stork."

I said, "Manny, that's a pelican."

He said, "It is? I thought it was a stork."

I said, "You better get off this reservation so you can figure out the difference between a pelican and a stork. You better go to a zoo somewhere."

He said, "How are we going to have a baby if this is a pelican?"

I said, "You're my entertainment committee, you know that?"

He said, "Brenda, this is a flamingo." Well, as soon as he said it I knew that's what it was, and felt a little stupid, and mad at him, how he was always just playing me, and wouldn't have talked to him all the rest of that morning, but then he came over and squatted in front of me. He put his elbows on his knees and held his face like a little boy. He said that maybe we should pawn that flamingo for a stork so we could have a baby, and I said, "Okay by me."

Except when he was drinking, just about anything Manny said was okay by me. Not that I'd let him know this. I'm not just a go-along sort of person. What I believe in is timing. I mean, you keep a guy guessing, but the timing has got to be right. Once, I guess we'd been on the reservation a year or so. I thought Manny was starting to like me, and I decided to test him. I was supposed to meet him in my front yard, and we were going to get up a game of softball. He was late. I knew he'd expect me to be waiting. What I did was just put the ball in the yard, then I ran in the house. This was so I could see his face when he came to meet me. You know you're getting to a guy depending on how his face looks when he's expecting to find you someplace but you're not there. I hid behind the curtains in our front room, and after a while Manny showed up. The ball was in the middle of the front lawn. He stood over that ball, then stooped down, picked it up, started tossing it up, catching it. And he walked off. Like he'd found a prize, like that ball was all he was after in the first place. He never glanced at the house.

I figured my timing was off. He didn't like me well enough yet to miss me. And after he left me for good, I figured my timing had been off the whole time I knew Manny, and maybe there wasn't such a thing as timing at all.

Manny came home one morning carrying a foreman's white hard hat under his arm. I said, "You get a promotion?" He said my dad had been for a three A.M. visit to the roaster room at the mill and forgot his hat when he left. Manny also said that he thought a man should spend a lot of time with his wife and from here on we would be spending a lot of time together.

Then he went and hung the hard hat on a peg in the living room.

Manny stayed home nights after my dad caught him drinking at the mill. He didn't sleep. He said he couldn't shake that night-shift habit, but I think it was the liquor, the way it keeps you awake. He'd want me to stay up with him to keep him company. "We'll sleep during the day," he'd say. I tried to, but I'm a night sleeper, and anyway, Manny didn't sleep day or night. He didn't sleep. I told him I needed to sleep. "Then fucking sleep!" he'd yell, and leave, sometimes for weeks, and then I'd have nightmares of him splattered on some highway, drunk in front of some off-reservation bar.

One night I woke up and Manny was sitting by the side of my bed. He'd been gone maybe a month, and at first I was glad to see him, but then I noticed he was weird. He was talking to me about the Navajos in World War II, how they used Navajo for a code language, and after a while he wasn't making any sense. "And Brenda, them Nazis couldn't break it because it wasn't written, how about that, we never thought to write it down, and my cousin Suzanne went to Deermont and she said there were no boys, how about that, but she liked it anyway and never came home to the reservation, she went to Paris or Spain drinking tequila, Indians shouldn't drink, Brenda, like your dad says, because we have type B blood and you have type A . . ."

I mean, it was weird waking up to his talk, and his eyes were dead—they didn't see me. I said his name over and over: "Manny, Manny, Manny—Manuelito!"

"Was a drunk," he said. He laughed.

I said, "Manny, why do you drink?"

He said, "To get drunk."

I left the bedroom. He yelled after me, "And I don't want to be talked out of it."

I went to the kitchen to make coffee. In the kitchen I found a puddle on the floor. It was urine. Manny came into the kitchen. He stared at the puddle on the floor, and then at me, foolishly, a little smile. He said, "I don't think I'm responsible for that."

My heart was cold. You don't ever really know a person, and maybe it's just those childhood games that make you think you do—you try to remember how he used to look, but all you know is how he looks when he drinks. It's not like a country song. It's not the good and then the bad, and how it gives you a reason to sing. It's that you don't know a person. He was a goddamn drunk and I was a goddamn drunk's wife and it was just piss on the floor.

He left that night for good, and good riddance is what I said to him, but he was in my head. Like a bad dream, but worse, because I was nothing but scared most of the time living with Manny—still after he left I only remembered I was scared but couldn't remember how it felt. And that's a bad dream, when you know good and well somebody's a drunk. I never thought he'd leave me for good. I'd watch for him sometimes—at night when I couldn't sleep. I'd go sit with that plastic pink stork that I kept in the living room, just like it was a real thing. Funny, huh? With all the lights off, me and this bird; maybe we were watching for a face in the window. Manny said that if a Navajo witch comes for you, you'll see a painted white face in the window. Then he said I didn't have to worry since I wasn't Navajo. Still, I'd watch that window and think how a Navajo skinwalker *could* witch a white. How things get in your head, and you can't get them out. You can't sleep for thinking about something.

Then a couple of days ago they called me from a detoxification center in Farmington and said they'd picked up Manny. He had to detoxify for a few days, then he could go, but they wouldn't let him go on his own recognizance because he was a danger to himself. I said to tell him I wasn't his wife anymore. Then I said never mind, I would do it myself.

There is a women's ward and a men's ward in the center. The walls of both are painted green. The whole place smells like vomit. In each ward there are rows of cot-size beds lined against the walls, and in most beds lumps that are people sleeping, although some of the people are sitting in bed smoking and others are walking around. There is a young black-haired woman who lies flat on her back and yells to the ceiling, "Put the music on."

I hear Manny before I see him. When I turn the corner from the women's ward into the men's he's right there in the bunk closest to me, next to the wall. His hair is long, he wears a red bandanna around his forehead, and his pajamas are paisley. He doesn't sound drunk. I can't see his face. He's sitting on his bunk talking to the man next to him. The man is asleep.

Manny is saying, "So they took me to this center for detoxification, and I told them I'm no ordinary drunk Indian. I'm Todacheene, man. Bitterwater, and that don't mean whiskey, neither. Manuelito was Bitterwater.

"So, first thing they took my clothes, gave me pajamas with feet. Like kids wear, pajamas with feet, man. And the next thing, they processed me. That girl said, 'First thing we had to sober you up, boss.' Chester, I was twenty-four-hours dead drunk. That girl said I was being processed on the second day because I was dead drunk on the first. And she asked me, 'How old are you?' and I said, 'Old enough to know better.' What do you think of that, hey, Chester? And she asked me, 'When did you start to drink?' I told her, 'About two days ago.' I told her I am a social drinker, that I only drink socially. Chester, she's a smart chick. She said, 'Quit fooling around.'

"So I asked her, 'Who put feet in my pajamas?' She said, 'That's so you won't run away.' And I told her, man—'I can run with feet in my pajamas.' And she said, 'Yeah, but you'd look a little silly, don't you think?' What do you think of that, man?

"Hey—look here, Chester. It's my wife."

"I'm not your wife anymore, Manny."

Manny scoots back on the bed. He says, "That's okay." He pats the mattress beside him. He says, "Have a sit-down."

From his bunk we can see the glassed-in nurses' station and two Navajo nurses watching us. There is also a white man. Manny says he drives the drunkmobile.

Manny introduces me to Chester.

I say, "Manny, he's drunk. He's passed out and can't hear you."

Manny stares at his hands in his lap. He says quietly, "I know that." We both stare at his long fingers, and the skin is peeling around the nails. "I'm just trying to make it interesting for him." The fingernails are white and look cold. His hands look very cold. He yells so everybody in the room can hear, "I'm just trying to make things interesting for my bedmate here." The Navajo nurses squint at us.

I take Manny's left hand and put it between my hands, but they are too small, so I put it under my thigh to warm it.

Manny is staring at his feet. He says, "You know, these pajamas didn't always have feet. Somebody sewed them on there. Who do you think is responsible for that?"

I don't know.

He says, "If you were still my wife, I'd ask you to do something."

"What."

"To cut the feet out of these pajamas."

"You'd just go get drunk again."

Manny leans his head back against the wall and closes his eyes. He says, "Maybe." He sticks his right hand under his own thigh to warm it. He says, "Maybe not."

starburst

arry Deemer watches his wife, Rosy, across the deck. She's talking to Scott Wentworth while Scott grills ribs. The rhinestone barrette in Rosy's hair catches the sun and directs an oval ray onto the Wentworths' redwood siding. The ray seesaws over one chunk of boards. It's Janet Wentworth's barrette. A couple of weeks earlier, when Janet first noticed her missing barrette in Rosy Deemer's hair, she advised Barry to check into it.

Rosy leans backwards against the deck railing, her elbows propped on the top beam, and seems amused by the barbecue proceedings—there's that little half-smile. She tells Scott to be a sport. She tells him she's only asking a half-hour of his time. "Barry won't do it," she says loudly, making sure Barry hears. Rosy wants Scott to dress up like a gorilla and deliver balloons to a birthday party at the Top Deck Lounge that night. Rosy has a little balloon-gram business, and the gorilla-grams are popular. They have other grams as well—a leprechaun on St. Patty's, cupid on Valentine's Day—but the gorilla is requested the most.

"You're out of your gourd," Scott says. "Isn't she out of her gourd, Barry?"

"A little rambunctious," Barry says.

The barrette holds Rosy's gray streak. It's silver, really—just the one streak on her entire head. She laughs at something Scott says that Barry can't quite hear. Then they both laugh.

Once, Rosy took an avocado—the first time they went out. They'd stopped at the Safeway for picnic supplies, then headed for the La Platas. Halfway through the meal Rosy pulled from her windbreaker pocket an avocado that hadn't gone through the checkout. She didn't crack a smile. She reached in her jeans for her Swiss Army knife, flipped the blade, halved the avocado, then quartered it, then halved the quarters—all with neat incisions, as if she were performing an operation—and peeled the skin back, making eight perfect crescents. She ate the entire avocado. When she was finished, she asked him if he was going to bust her.

At the time, he had thought it was an isolated incident, but now there's this barrette. Barry can see the headlines: COP'S WIFE A KLEPTOMANIAC.

Rosy tells Scott that he'll get to dance with the birthday girl. Scott brushes the last coat of sauce over the ribs; some drips on the coals and they hiss. "The band always spotlights the birthday girl. See, they black out first, then the gorilla comes up the stairs, and they have a red light on him and a white light on her. It's great."

"It's a disease," Janet whispers in Barry's ear. She is sitting next to Barry on the picnic bench, stirring sugar into her iced tea. "It's like alcoholism. They can't help themselves, and neither can kleptos."

Barry thinks Rosy helps herself pretty good. "She's just trying to be cute," he says.

"They don't even want what they go after. Usually."

"She's just trying to be funny."

"They're capable of anything—the really bad ones are."

He knows Rosy is capable of anything.

"Did you go through her drawers?"

After Janet told him about the barrette, Barry did a little research. He read in the police dossiers about the case of an army officer's wife who stockpiled underwear that she'd lifted from other army officers' wives. At parties she'd slip into their bedrooms and take samples from lingerie drawers: briefs and bikinis—cotton, silk, nylon. Finally, one woman got wise; she began investigating lingerie drawers at parties. In one house she found a bureau full of underwear she recognized and hundreds of pairs she didn't.

Rosy's case is not the same. This is jewelry. Still, Barry went through her drawers just to see. He found more than he expected, but nothing he didn't recognize: pairs and pairs of white cotton briefs folded in little triangles. Barry counted them—nineteen. What did one woman need with nineteen pairs of underpants? He checked the labels: all Jockey. And the T-shirts were L.L.Bean T-shirts, and there were two slips—no frills, a little worn—and pantyhose folded in squares, a tan satin bra, a shiny white one, a couple of pairs of long underwear: a no-nonsense lingerie drawer, exactly what you'd expect from a country girl in a cold climate. And the sock drawer was exactly what you'd expect as well; he had dug through wool socks, mounds of them, grays and whites. He didn't know what he was looking for, but he knew it wouldn't be gray or white.

At dinner the talk turns to badgers. Scott says that as far as he is concerned the badger menace is escalating, the population on the bluff exploding, the whole damn prairie teeming with burrowing mammals. "Little sons of bitches, Barry—I see them on the hill." He squints at the hill that is his backyard. The Wentworth house is halfway up the western bluff, one of the highest human habitats in Farmington. Barry patrols the bluffs when things are slow, driving along one dirt road or another up there, just following where it leads. If you head east along the edge, you'll see all of Farmington to the south, miles of just nothing north.

"They're mean animals," Scott says.

"They'll stand you off," Barry says.

"I know it."

"Scott's at his wits' end," Janet says.

"Thing is you get five feet from them, they'll stand there and spit in your face," Scott says.

"Just eyeball them," Rosy says. She is piling sour cream on her potato. So far she has piled four spoonfuls.

"This is not a little threat," Scott informs her. "They won't just rout garbage." Scott doesn't look at Rosy when he says this. Throughout dinner Barry has kept an eye on the barrette; Janet has kept her eye on the barrette; Rosy has kept one hand on the barrette. Scott has not looked at Rosy—he has taken, Barry thinks, extra care not to look at Rosy. Barry wonders why.

Scott says he wants the Farmington police department to bomb the badger holes with chemicals.

"It's not so easy," Barry says. "We bomb one hole, we're as good as killing off half a mile of the animal population."

"I tell you, I'm going to take a gun to the next one that gets in the garden."

"Go ahead." Barry grins.

Janet asks if the cops would look the other way, and Barry says, "I'll bust his ass."

"It's not just one, I'm telling you," Scott says. "Barry, they'll go after small animals."

"What you do, sucker them. Manipulate them outside the city limits, and you'll be within your rights as far as the firearms code goes."

Scott says he doesn't see how he is going to manipulate them outside the city limits, the way they'll just spit in your face. He's worried about rabies. Just one with rabies could infect countless small domestic animals. And they are enterprising sons of bitches, he continues—he points out again that they don't go for just garbage.

"They are little thieves," Rosy agrees. She smiles at the skin of what had been her potato. "The badger is a little thief."

When he went through Rosy's drawers, Barry told himself that it was more of a scavenger hunt than search and seizure, not so different from scavenging loot when he was a kid. From the ages of ten to twelve Barry and Scott organized scavenger hunts to gather booty around the neighborhood. The two were always divided in strategies. Scott said loot wasn't loot unless you sneaked it pure and simple, but Scott was not a very complicated fellow. There were ways to steal and ways to steal. Barry liked the "It's your civic duty" approach. During scavenger hunts he'd knock on a neighbor's door and present a list of items needed by the New Mexico Children's Home, although at the time he was not even sure that such a home existed. In spite of himself, Barry had to admire the Rosy Deemer method—sneaking into your friend's bedroom, pilfering her rhinestone, then wearing it in the light of day; or palming an avocado when the cop's back is turned, then stripping and eating it right in his face. What do you do when she holds out eight perfect black crescents of avocado skin that curl like a witch's nails in the palms of her hands, opens her fingers, lets the peelings fall to the ground between you, grinds them in the dirt, and begins to stroke you: your upper arms, your neck, then your hair. What do you do? What Barry knows is the avocado was not a major crime. What he wonders is whether it is a symptom of some sickness.

Barry fell in love with Rosy when he was eleven years old.

Of course, he didn't notice her until the day he intercepted a note from Rosy to Scott that read, "Who do you like?" in Scott's pinched scrawl, and below it, in Rosy's galloping hand, "I like you. Why?" That's when he noticed her. He fell in love with her a few weeks later, when he saw her in her backyard, swinging on her swing set.

The swing set, ungrounded, inched across the lawn. Rosy had her eyes squeezed shut, and she was talking—a whisper, really, or a hiss. Barry recognized the words to a jump-rope rhyme he'd heard the girls sing on the playground, but Rosy chanted venomously, as if accusing the air she kicked with her swinging feet:

> Fudge, fudge, call the judge,
> Mama's got a newborn baby
> It ain't no girl and it ain't no boy
> It's just a newborn baby.
> Wrap it up in tissue paper,
> Send it down the elevator.
> First floor, stop.
> Second floor, stop.
> Third floor, kick it out the door,
> And you'll never see baby anymore.

Every time she said the word "stop" she stuck her legs straight to the sky, tilted her back parallel to the ground, and pumped with such a force that Barry thought she'd wind herself around the top bar of the swing set. The whole swing set bucked like a mad thing, and when she finally bailed out, she twisted in midair, landed cross-legged sitting on the ground, faced the swing, and clapped—she clapped at the empty swing. Barry laughed, although it wasn't really funny, that intent look on her face. He laughed. And Rosy fixed on him a wild, yellow-eyed animal look that made him feel as though *he* had been hurled down the elevator. He gagged on his laughter. Then the look was gone, replaced by befuddlement, as if he'd caught her in the bathroom, dancing naked before the mirror.

He said the only thing he could think to say: "You like Scott Wentworth."

And then it was Rosy's turn to laugh. She threw her head back and hooted at the swing. "That dope?"

"Then who do you like?"

She gave him a sly, furtive look. "I like you. Why?"

She may have liked Barry, but Rosy and Scott were an item from the time they were eleven years old until Scott joined the army at eighteen and married Janet six months later. The funny thing was, those years in the back of the room during Civics when Rosy passed notes to Scott but kept her eyes on Barry, when she danced slow dances with Scott, her chin digging into his shoulder but her eyes on Barry, he wondered if maybe she did like him, if maybe she didn't think Scott really was a dope (which he was). He wondered if it had been deliberate, that long adolescent dance with Scott Wentworth, a way of courting and teasing and seducing Barry Deemer without ever touching him, a slow angling, worth the wait—to let him know she was worth the wait.

He and Rosy had been married ten years. He wondered why he still wondered about these things. He wondered where she got the barrette. Did she steal the barrette, or did Scott give it to her?

Rosy is chewing on little bits of meat stuck in the grooves of a rib. She asks Scott which weapon he would use on badgers in the garden, and Scott says he figures his little .30-caliber Luger would do it, but Rosy disagrees; she'd use a .45 or nothing. "Isn't that right, sweetheart?" she says.

"You want to be sure," Barry says.

"Unless you're right up on them. If you're close enough to get a starburst, then a Luger would work," Rosy says.

Janet asks what a starburst is, and Rosy, who has always taken an avid interest in police work, explains that it's a gunpowder-residue pattern from a bullet wound. The pattern will change depending on the distance from weapon to target, stability, and bullet path. They analyze the residue pattern to help reconstruct the circumstances of a crime, she says. A starburst indicates close range, so every suicide is a starburst.

"Although the starburst does not always limit your options, does it, sweetheart?" Rosy goes on. "There are factors you can't image. Dust. Corrosion on the inside of the barrel. This guy shot his wife from a distance of twenty feet, but they only knew because the guy confessed later. At first they thought it was a suicide, because there was a clear starburst pattern. It turned out that the gun had been sitting around for forty years—forty years of accumulated crud went with the bullet and happened to form a starburst." Rosy pushes her plate away and smiles at Janet. "You can't be sure about anything unless you can duplicate the exact circumstances of a crime."

Scott asks Janet if she made a lemon pie for dessert. Janet is watching the sprinkler in the backyard. It is sputtering—a tiny fountain in the middle of the lawn; she's staring as though this were a fascinating object. Janet is twenty-eight but looks eighteen. Her skin is that ivory white, without a laugh line or blemish; she looks like she'd bruise if you put thumb pressure to her, and she has watery blue eyes, clear in the whites because she doesn't drink. "Barry, she's a dancer," Scott had told him over the phone the night before he married Janet. "She's got everything." And she moves like a dancer. And the clothes she wears—short denim skirts with tennis shoes and thin little sleeveless cotton blouses unbuttoned halfway down so you can see a lace camisole, where if Rosy wore blouses like that you'd see a bra. And you can talk to Janet. She has been nothing but nice about the barrette.

Rosy is studying the side of Janet's face. She says, "Did you know, Janet, that the police investigating team uses cadavers to duplicate the exact circumstances of a crime?" Rosy looks at Barry. She is lying. They don't do that anymore, and Rosy knows it.

Barry looks away. He watches the table move. Scott's leg is jumping up and down—he's got this nervous habit, and the picnic table twitches with the leg. Janet's fingers, white-nailed from pressure, grip her fork. Janet would probably rather not hear talk about shooting holes in cadavers, which is why Rosy goes on about it. She knows Janet gets squeamish.

"What they do is dress a cadaver like the victim," Rosy goes on. "Say a victim is wearing a sheepskin coat. You dress the corpse in sheepskin of the same thickness, duplicate the ammo, and *whammy*."

A bald-faced lie. She has them completely conned. And when she isn't making things up, she's got this trick of making you wonder. Barry thinks of the first time he saw Rosy naked. It was clear they were going to sleep together, and she excused herself and went into the bathroom and came out naked. Maybe it was a stupid thing, because she got that funny, confused look she gets, but he said, "That girl's bare-assed naked." That was all. It had been a good first night, a fine first night. But the next day he saw the line in a notebook she'd left conspicuously open on her desk, just the one line with that day's date: "That girl's bare-assed naked." What did she mean by writing it down? He couldn't get it out of his head. And what was in his head at the time he'd said it, and what was in hers? He couldn't get the notebook out of his head, which made him realize right away that Rosy would be an asset to any interrogation team, the way she had him guessing and made him think he was a chump for even paying attention.

Barry pushes away from the table, picks up his empty plate, and carries it into the house. He heads upstairs, where the bathroom is, and switches on the light, but he doesn't go into the bathroom. The Wentworths' bedroom door is ajar. He walks down the hall and pushes on it. The room is over the deck and the window is open, so Barry can hear Rosy clearly, almost as if he were standing on top of her. She is saying that the cadavers are usually prisoners who die in jail. She sounds like an authority; she sounds delighted with herself. Barry moves straight to the bureau. There are two jewelry boxes, one at each end of the bureau, and Barry opens the box on the left. There's nothing but rhinestones, which surprises him— rhinestone pins and earrings and two necklaces. Barry rifles through the colored glass. As far as he can see, Rosy got the pick of the lot. Then he opens the box on the right and is surprised again. This stuff looks real. There's a pearl necklace, a ring with red stones, maybe some rubies. The ring looks old. Rosy was just trying to be cute. She didn't take anything valuable. Rosy was just trying to be funny.

Unless Scott gave her the barrette. Why would Scott give Rosy junk when there was this? Because Scott was two-bit. Barry saw this kind of thing all the time. Petty thieves who figured minor infractions would go unnoticed.

Barry hears Scott ask Rosy how they could simulate a moving target. "They put it on rollers," she says. "Silhouette rollers, like the kind they use at shooting ranges." Another lie. Rosy took that barrette. Scott didn't give her the rhinestone, and the only question is why she took junk.

Barry closes the jewelry box. He opens the top bureau drawer. It is Janet's underwear drawer. Silks, mostly, from what he can tell. Spaghetti-strap silk undershirts and matching bikinis. Some lace stuff, strips of lace—G-strings, stockings with sequins. It is definitely a more interesting drawer than Rosy's.

Barry takes from Janet's lingerie drawer a pair of blue underpants; they feel like silk. He walks over to the window. Rosy is leaning across the picnic table, telling Scott and Janet more lies about what the police do. Barry wants her to look up. He wants her to see him looking at her. "And this is the reason I know you shouldn't shoot badgers with that little Luger," she is saying. "See, sometimes, instead of using a cadaver, what they'll do is try to find a live animal and shoot it. Say, a jackrabbit, and—"

"That makes me sick," Janet says. Her face is flushed. Barry crushes the underwear, then lets his fist relax. He rubs the grooves in the waistband, then traces the elastic around the legs. He imagines Janet in the blue silk.

"And what they found," Rosy says, "is that even after ten shots from a gun the caliber of your Luger a jackrabbit won't always drop. But if you use a Colt forty-five or a Winchester, you'll drop it in three. This only applies if you don't hit a vital organ first."

"You're kidding! That makes me sick," Janet says. Barry feels for her, the way Rosy will push and push.

But then Rosy leans back, and when she speaks her voice is different. "Oh, Christ," she says. She has dropped an octave. "Of course it makes *you* sick, Janet."

"They're just killing those animals!" Janet says. She does not look at Rosy. Janet looks at the ground. Rosy stares at the side of Janet's face; she looks exasperated. She can't believe that Janet is buying this.

"How else are you going to simulate?" Rosy asks.

"Who would want to?" Janet says.

"Hey, calm down," Scott says. He gets up and walks to the barbecue; he begins scraping the grill with the spatula.

Rosy continues staring at the side of Janet's face, but Janet doesn't look up. Nobody looks up. On the deck no one speaks. Rosy begins peeling bits of label off the ketchup bottle. She looks tired. Behind her the Farmington bluffs are turning blue and the sun rests on the plain. Barry knows it is her least favorite time of the day. She says that the day feels too close at dusk, as if the scenery is moving in—you go outside and the air has the feel of your own breath.

Barry holds the underwear loosely—it's like tissue, hardly any weight at all—and he wonders if Rosy has ever worn silk. "It doesn't matter what you wear," she said once. "Within fifteen minutes of getting dressed in the morning, your body no longer feels your clothes. You get numb." Barry closes his eyes. On the inside of his lids, he sees moving red suns. He opens his eyes. Rosy is studying Scott's face like it's a problem. Scott scrapes the grill.

"So," Rosy says at last. She leans back on the bench. "So are you going to be the gorilla or what!" Scott laughs and looks at Janet. Janet is watching the bluffs. "Come on, it'll be fun."

Scott stares at his wife for a minute. Finally he shrugs. "Hell, I guess I'm game," he says.

Rosy laughs. "Good. You'll come, won't you, Janet?" Janet says no. "You'll be sorry," Rosy says. "It'll be a gas." She grins at Scott. Then she says, "I wonder where Barry's gotten to."

Barry steps away from the window. He walks to the dresser, where the lingerie drawer is still open. He drops the underwear in the drawer. He stares at it. Then he picks it up again and puts it in his pocket. He shuts the drawer and goes downstairs.

The Top Deck is dark except for the neon beer signs. One of the band members directs a red spotlight onto the stairway. The drummer has muffled his snare to make it sound like a tom-tom, and the female singer shakes a rattle. The first thing Barry sees is the bouquet of balloons, multicolored, floating up the stairs. Then the spot widens to include the gorilla. A female voice in the room says, "Oh, God," and a group at one of the tables laughs.

The gorilla looks fierce enough in the red light—the widow's peak, the pronounced nostrils, the mouth like a blunted, downturned snout—and Barry can see the canines, probably bigger than a normal gorilla has.

"He should bend over," Rosy whispers. "He should stomp or something."

Another spotlight comes on, a white one that shines on a girl who probably just turned twenty-one. She wears jeans, a red tank top, and three little braids in her hair. She's laughing hard and keeps saying, "How embarrassing!"

The gorilla bows to the birthday girl and offers her the balloons. "He looks ridiculous," Barry says, and Rosy laughs. The gorilla offers his hand and walks the birthday girl to the dance floor. The band begins to play, the vocalist sings, and everybody in the room cracks up:

> Can I have this dance for the rest of my life,
> Will you be my partner every night?

The song ends. Scott takes his mask off and dances a second time with the girl. Scott is a fair dancer. They country-swing to "I'll Be Your Baby Tonight."

Rosy says, "You know, a guy's got an obligation to ask a girl to dance."

Barry doesn't say anything, and Rosy begins shredding the label on her Michelob bottle. They watch through the set. Scott takes turns dancing with all the women at the birthday girl's table. He looks like he's having a terrific time.

"I could dance with Scott," Rosy says.

"Go ahead," Barry says. Rosy continues peeling the label.

Barry props his feet on the chair next to him. There is a distinctive odor to this place, a metallic smell of liquor gone stale and of cigarettes—like poor-quality wet aluminum that you can tear with your fingers. Barry has smelled the same odor on winos, and it seems funny to him how a human being at his most human, a human being ungroomed, will come to have that almost clean smell of cheap metal.

In the dim light, the rhinestone barrette looks like a band of black hair bisecting Rosy's silver streak. She seems to have forgotten it. She plays with bits of paper from her beer bottle and watches the dancers. After a while she says, "Where'd you go tonight?"

"Tonight?"

"While we were eating, where'd you go?"

Barry puts his hand in his pocket. He says, "Where'd you get the barrette?"

Rosy grins, like she's been waiting for somebody to ask that question all night. "I found it," she says.

"Yeah?" Barry says. "You want to know what I found?"

"What?"

He says, "You didn't find that barrette."

Rosy puts her arm around him and her chin on his right shoulder. She whispers, "So are you going to bust me?"

Barry looks out at the room. Scott's gorilla head, in the middle of the birthday table, scowls at the empty beer bottles. Barry laughs. "Now that's one mean monkey," he says. He twists the panties in his pocket, then pulls them out and drops them on the floor. Later he might tell Rosy that he stole a pair of Janet's underpants and then left them for the barmaid. Rosy will appreciate that. He figures that's his job — keeping it interesting for her. But now he pushes his chair back from the table and stands up. He asks his wife if she would like to dance.

billy by the bay

The boss told Billy he was no damn good, and he told him he was fired. He said, "Billy, git on out of here, and don't you come back." Billy got out with his knife.

It was his birthday. At midnight he would be twenty-four years old.

In the parking lot there were scores of cars Billy didn't recognize and one he did. The Camaro he'd barfed in, and slept in, and ridden halfway across the country in. The boss's car. The car was parked in its regular slot.

Billy sidled up to it. The car had radials and a hundred percent of its tread. Billy thought of the bouncer and looked back at the door. The bouncer was sitting on his bench, huddled up in a furry-hooded parka, blowing on his hands. Pretty girls with spiked heels were huddled around him, begging to get in free. Tonight, Billy had had his chance at a pretty girl. Billy's balls were golden birthday balls tonight, and Sally had offered to touch them before midnight. Sally Raleigh. Sally said she would be the last woman to touch them in his twenty-third and the first in his twenty-fourth. Sally Rally, Rally Sally, say it fast—ooh, Billy was drunk.

But his balls hadn't been touched, wouldn't be touched now, not in his twenty-third year, maybe not in his twenty-fourth, either. Billy squatted down next to the Camaro. He tried to remember the last time they had been touched. Certainly since he was a little thumbprint in his mother's fist. Certainly since then, but just now he couldn't remember when or who—all he could remember was Sally Rally and her promise. He slipped the knife in the tire. He pulled it out. Air sirened through the crack, and Billy plugged it with his fingers, "Shh, shh."

The bouncer was blowing on his hands. The pretty girls had gone on in, and the band was playing "Sissy Strut."

Billy began to crawl among the cars. He held his knife between his teeth. He wanted to cut more tires. It felt good cutting them and listening to the air hiss out, though he also wanted to sleep, to go on home, but he would have to catch a taxi now that the boss's tires were cut and Billy was fired anyway. Even if the tires weren't cut, he wouldn't give Billy a ride home, nor lift a finger to help him in spite of everything, in spite of how Billy was his personal pack rat, his toady roadie, how Billy carried his damn drums in and his damn drums out, in and out, in and out of every gig—*Carry my drums, Billy, and I'll teach you how to play*—in and out of every gig and set them up while he did his glad-handing, his *How-you-doings* and *Looking-goods* . . .

Billy forgot the rug. Tonight, Billy forgot the rug on which the drums were supposed to be set, the good-luck rug. Why was it Billy's responsibility to remember the rug? It wasn't his good luck. Anyway, he remembered the drums. Yes, he did, he always remembered the drums.

All along the fence behind the bar, smokers leaned out toward the bay. Billy crawled among the cars closest to the smokers and he took the caps off tire valves. He poked the little buttons in the valves with the tip of his knife. Each time a smoker spoke, he poked, and air hissed, and when they stopped speaking, he stopped. The smokers were saying pitiful things to each other, things like, "Food makes me happy."

A rat slid over the cement just beyond the smokers' feet. Billy's skin crawled. Where there was one rat, there would be two. He turned around and stared at the dumpster behind him and saw rats, hundreds of them swarming the dumpster. Even though he knew he wasn't really seeing them, he knew he really was, because what you don't see is what's real, WHAT YOU DON'T SEE IS WHAT'S REAL. Billy wanted to scream. Mostly all he ever wanted to do was scream, scream, scream, in churches and movie theaters and at the DMV and in libraries and on buses—

But who would want to touch his balls then? If all he did was scream?

Tonight he'd watched a seafaring vessel dock among the piers. This was a mammoth of a boat. A president of a boat that stretched half the length of the pier, one hundred percent steel from stern to prow, and Billy had thought, *What if I lived on such a boat?* Tonight, at sunset, he had stood there, himself, among the smokers, and he watched the boat dock, and he knew with certainty that one day he would be the captain of a great big ship, and he told Sally all about it, and Sally put her arm around him. She said, "Billy, when you're the captain of that ship, I'm going off my diet. We're going to have us a party. We'll invite the fish, and we'll eat 'em. We'll be fair. We'll eat black fish and white fish and every colored fish there is." And she said, "This is your night, Billy. You can do anything you want—to me."

That was before the boss told Billy he would never be anything but a third-rate roadie who lost the hardware and broke the skins. Said nobody would ever let him play on a gig, and the only reason he let him carry the drums was because he felt sorry for his sorry ass. Said it to Billy's face on his birthday with Sally Rally standing by, her dress riding low on her tits, tits on display in a help-yourself minute.

It occurred to Billy right now, glimpsing the big ship just beyond this car's bumper, that he would kill the drummer tonight. In an instant Billy's blood turned to quicksilver and he laughed through his teeth.

Billy began to crawl back along the cold cement, through cigarette butts and broken glass, toward the Camaro, and as he crawled he whispered, "Could and would, could and would," through the knife in his teeth.

Just then, people started pouring out of the club, coatless people fanning themselves, glistening throats in the club's neon light. Billy could hear the boss tapping the snare and talking through the microphone, "Don't go away. Be right back. Pause for the cause—"

Billy skittered into the shadows behind the Camaro. He was cold, shivering cold. He felt as if rats were creeping up his neck. He didn't want this moment to turn sour. Every other moment this goddamn year had turned from sweet to sour—*Here's our Billy-come-later*—before he knew it, before he could do a thing—*Tell you what, if you can't come in on the beat, please don't come in at all*—sweet to sour—*Better late than never, hey Billy? Billy's off in la-la land*—because he always thought first and acted second—*Because you are a MENTAL PERSON! You couldn't find the pocket if you fell into it. Don't think about it, JUST DO IT, BILLY!*

Billy always thought about it and then the moment turned, sweet to sour.

The boss and his brother, Louis, had come out and were walking toward the Camaro. Louis was fishing in his pocket.

"Did you see that girl?" the boss said. They stopped in front of the car.

"The one who almost fell on me?" Louis pulled out his sawed-off, drilled-out piano key. He began cleaning the key with wire.

"Fine sense of balance." The boss laughed, and Louis laughed, too.

"I thought I was a dead man," Louis said. He began packing the piano-key pipe with weed.

"I thought you was smoked, you *and* the piano."

"What she's carrying around—" Louis said.

"You and the pi-ana and the floor."

"What she's carrying around," Louis said, "how does she keep from falling over?" He passed the pipe, held his lighter to it.

"I've seen her fall over," the boss said. He dragged on the pipe. "*Mm, hmm.*" He held his breath in his throat. "And when she falls—she bounces."

Louis laughed.

"*Ba-boom, ba-b-b-b-boom.* Don't take no applications," the boss hollered into the night. "We got us a bouncer!" He dragged on the pipe. The sweet smell wafted back to Billy.

That dress was about to fall off of her," Louis said. "I didn't know they made 'em that big. Good-looking lady, though."

Billy plugged his ears. He didn't want to hear them talk about the good-looking lady. In his head, Billy sang, "La-la-la-la-la-la," so he wouldn't have to hear who they were talking about, and he whispered "la-la-la-la-la-la-la" just under his breath—

"What was it she was saying to you?" Louis said. "I saw her talking to you."

"She promised me affection. She said, 'This is your night, boy. You can do anything you want to me.'"

La-la-la-la—Billy would like to do something to him. Billy would like to—Billy would like to—Billy's eyes were fog-fuzzed headlights. Under the neon, the pencil-legged girls hiked their skirts and flexed their butts and Billy would like to, he would like to—feed them, feed them, feed them unspecified food for a long time, unspecified food right in front of God, right up there onstage, feed them, fill them up, their arms and legs and toes and ears and nostrils and hair follicles for a long time and every time they cried, "I'm full!" Billy'd feed them some more until they split right open and their cardboard blood came spitting out, their—

"Hey, you guys," a woman yelled. "My tire's flat! Hey, all these tires are flat!"

Billy ducked down. He crouched, hugging his knees. Air whistled through his teeth. "HEY!" a woman yelled, and Billy dove under the Camaro's bumper, rolled to the Chevy next door, scooted on to the Nissan. People were shouting about their flat tires, and Billy's blood was thudding in his ears. He rolled and crawled, rolled and crawled to the chainlink fence, closed and padlocked, but Billy was skinny, a whisper in the night, and he squirmed through the gap underneath the lock. "Billy! Goddamn you, Billy!" He squirmed and ran down the pier toward the boat, his own name thudding in his ears.

The pier, moon-white under the fluorescents, his skinny legs fluttering in the cold: Billy was laughing, zigzagging down the way, and behind him, fatter people were climbing the fence. "BIL-LY!" they all screamed.

Birthday Billy, you scoundrel! He laughed, but he was screaming, too, in his head, because he had done it again. Let the moment pass. What had he been thinking? And the man just under his thumb.

The sour stench of rotten plank rose under his feet. There was nothing to run to. At the end of the pier, a wall of lonely steel was docked ten feet from solid ground. A ship. A monster of a ship that was so far out of reach it might as well be on the moon. And a bay. A frigid bay full of rats and *don't you come back*. Billy ran. As he ran his granite birthday balls flopped between his legs. "Could and would, could and would!" he sang. Behind him, somebody was keeping time. Tic-toc, tic-toc, at the stroke of the clock the time will be—

But Billy was running, not thinking at all, and then he was leaping over the inky water of San Francisco Bay, right smack-dab into the middle of one sweet moment.